Solo Spinout

Stories and a Novella

Also by Ann Nietzke

Windowlight
Natalie on the Street

Solo Spinout

Stories and a Novella

Ann Nietzke

"Solo Spinout" first appeared in *Shenandoah*, vol. 42, no. 2 (summer 1992).
"Los Angeles Here and Now" first appeared in *Other Voices*, vol. 6, no. 19 (fall 1993).
"Jarring Light" first appeared in the *Massachusetts Review*, vol. 36, no. 2 (summer 1995).

Published by
Soho Press, Inc.
853 Broadway
New York, NY 10003

Library of Congress Cataloging in Publication Data

Nietzke, Ann, 1945–
  Solo spinout : stories and a novella / Ann Nietzke.
    p. cm.
  Contents: Solo spinout—Los Angeles here and now—Jarring light—
No man's land.
  ISBN 1-56947-052-9 (alk. paper)
  I. Title.
PS3564.I36S6   1996
813'.54—dc20   95-47335
                                                    CIP

0/38

The author is deeply grateful for support and nurturance from the National Endowment for the Arts and the MacDowell Colony.

For
Jean Samuel

Contents

Solo Spinout

.

Lili intends not to stare at her clothes in the dryer but finds them more beguiling there than on hangers or herself, the way they tumble and twist back over each other, cacophonies of color. Everything she wears now is cotton, so the whole closet eventually winds its way into this randomly choreographed kind of scrutiny. These days she favors a certain intensity of hues, not bright, necessarily, but offbeat and solid. She has given up on dry cleaners, and she gave up ironing decades ago, halfway through a short early marriage. Wrinkled cotton must make its own statement, though she's at a loss now for glib explanations.

Underwear appears to be the morning's major motif, pink and peach and lavender bikinis from Sears. She buys them twenty-one at a time so she's seldom absolutely forced to the laundromat. Today she is wearing baggy jeans and a flowery print blouse she remembers buying at Goodwill ten or twelve years ago. And she is not wearing underwear—all the underwear is floating behind hot glass, including three pair of Garrett's jockey shorts, stunningly visible as the only bit of white in any of her loads. These shorts were buried like mines at the bottom of the basket, one detail he neglected in packing. Gone off, he has, after nearly eight years, for a bit of young skirt, a phrase Lili heard on PBS Sunday night and considers as good as any to cover such hackneyed and bitterly predictable behavior in a man of forty-eight. Sometimes she nearly gags with disappointment at him, aside from all the rest. Wash your dirty laundry in public, exactly the purpose for which laundromats are designed. "Speed Queens," not "Kings," the machines are called.

There is a jagged red wine stain from months ago on her right inner thigh, and Lili remembers hanging the jeans up dirty because they were too big even then (food had lost its appeal soon after the bit of skirt exerted hers). She cannot think when she ever washed this blouse, though of course she must have sometime over its years of use as last-ditch laundry-day apparel.

One wizened and grainy old señora she has seen here more than once wears five or six white cancans beneath her gaily dyed washday skirt, which she always removes and tosses into her load of darks just before she shuts the lid. The woman is not shy about this, managing to act fully clothed, even exuberant, in her layered slips until she can finally fish the garment out of the dryer and ease it on warm before immersing herself into a peculiarly elaborate ritual of fluff and fold. Lili thinks of removing the flowered blouse, walking slowly, bare-breasted, with it to the crude corner sink for a rinse and squeeze, sneaking it into somebody's dryer, and standing, arms folded, to watch it spin. She has tried to gaze at other people's dryers before but finds they fail to mesmerize. Are the bedsheets of strangers inherently dull and ugly or just uncharged by association.

She has been observing a young Hispanic woman with two brutally fresh suck marks along the side of her slender throat. At ease the girl exudes an air of defeat, but she has paraphernalia that keeps her quite busy at the washers, bleaches and softeners and whatnot, finally a two-foot length of unfinished wood that she uses to stir her clothes every few minutes, apparently suspicious of mechanical agitation. Lili imagines that with the blouse off she will be able to lick this woman's neck, lick across the bruises until there is some kind of shuddering.

In a moment, though, a young man, dark and hairy in his sleeveless white undershirt, can be seen peering through the side wall of glass. He cups his hands to shut out glare and spots his girl before she's aware of him. Lili watches him sneak up behind and whisper in her ear before he takes her hair in back and guides her mouth around to kiss. The stick in her hand makes this awkward and causes her to pull back, a bit abrupt in the face of such proprietorship. LAVADA 75¢, the sign behind them reads. SECADORAS SPEED QUEEN 25¢.

One quarter's worth of time is never enough and two is too much, unless you're stuck in the row of new dryers, where fifty cents falls short as well. Lili rebels against being taken advantage of this way and most often subverts the profit margin by dragging home damp clothes or insuring that another patron uses up her extra time. For now, the revolutions of her clothing, the hum and warmth of the machines, seem to be smoothing edges around her skin. She could turn down the heat and climb in with her towels, get a feel for buffeting, make a private rhythm, wrench the beat of the old duet. Suddenly a small-boned woman materializes beside her, urgently inquiring something Lili doesn't understand. *"No habla Español,"* she answers quickly, then sees the woman is Asian and backing away, so it must have been an attempt at English. "Ask me again," Lili calls out. "Come back and say it again." The woman turns and scurries off, and Lili feels a jab of regret halfway down her throat, convinced it was a question that she knows the answer to.

More and more there is danger in amber lights, something Lili has long believed and for which last week's accident was proof. Yellow means *floor it* now in L.A., but Lili suffered a moment of indecision, a failure of nerve, and found herself rear-ended at Fountain and Vermont, instantly heading west instead of north. Besides ruining her bumper and taillight, the impact blasted her radio full volume, so she kept hearing *solo spinout* in baritone off the traffic report. This amused her profusely once she got back home and opted to abandon the charade at work. She is claiming all her vacation time, purportedly setting things in order, eating Spoon-Size Shredded Wheat, relinquishing the entire clinic to Garrett and his little friend from Personnel, sparing them the inconvenience of avoiding her in Radiology, the snack bar, the employee lounge. Actually it was a *noninjury slammer* she was in, not a *solo spinout*. She seeks accounts of traffic deliberately now, finds them more enlightening and calming than music. *Traffic at a standstill, no cause apparent* feels illustrative. *Vehicle over the side with spectator slowing* seems to apply. In a *grand injury collision,* is it the bodily damage or the crash itself that's supposed to be so splendid? *The curiosity factor is causing a problem.*

Halfway down the room a balance buzzer sounds, and a stout, elegantly mustached Latino in a battered straw hat spreads himself quickly across the top of his washer, boots barely touching the floor, aiming to steady the violent shakes and muffle the banging side to side. The futility in this is soon apparent, and one whole section of the laundromat assumes a silent and unmistakable air of embarrassment and suspense. Just when Lili feels compelled to interfere and rearrange the gaucho's load, it snaps itself from spin to rinse. He slides off and regains his dignity, hope and stubbornness having won out over wisdom. Lili's car, she recalls, is due for significant brake work.

At Alpha Beta the cereal aisle seems to have lost its sedative power, the magical brand undistinguished today in a violent blur of boxes and labels. Lili's weary of it, anyhow, the way it sogs up in so little milk. In the parking lot a license plate read W8 4WIND, which has routed fragments of last night's exhausting dream, some bizarre and intricate business involving a dumbwaiter and pneumatic tubes at the clinic, where Lili was required to apply vague and complicated criteria for selecting X rays that would prove a point before the deadline. This meant spending hours in the basement file room, logging patient numbers and choosing specifically angled films, then rolling them tight so they'd fit the tubes to be sucked up into the building. Her supervisor Rhea stood by triple-checking each detail.

"Smile, dearie, it's good for the complexion." An elderly man is winking at her from the edge of the liquor department. Lili lifts her lip and shows him teeth, which appears to suffice, since he shuffles away. Her cart remains barren as she considers wines and whiskey. Up to the wreck, booze was doing its trick, but now she feels hung over as the first few sips go down. Still, she won't leave empty-handed—a gallon of gin will far outdistance any other buy. With the cereal off, there's no point to milk. Maybe shampoo and a fresh bar of soap. The red meats look too raw somehow, the chicken abhorrent yellow. Lili will purchase something already cooked, eat in the car if it comes to that. Even as a child she despised the boys who winked.

At the end of frozen foods, parked against the ice-cream case, an unattended, near-full cart is remarkable for what it lacks: paper and plastics, aluminum foil, cleansing agents, hygienic aids. This appears to be that rare phenomenon, a grocery cart devoted to food. Without hesitation Lili transfers her liquor and whirls the wire basket into a cash-only lane, heart pounding triumphant in perfect crime—the thrill and the goods without chargeable offense. From beneath three kinds of lettuce the checker lifts a double family-pack of pork chops, clean and cookable, Lili thinks, and possibly even edible. Maybe she can bake the squash as well. A package of five dozen flour tortillas floats by on the conveyor belt.

"Oh, my God," she laughs.

"Ma'am?" The kid at the register breaks his rhythm.

"What's this?" she asks, pointing to an aberrant sweet potato the size of a flattened grapefruit.

"That's jicama, ma'am."

"Which is what?" she presses.

"Just jicama, ma'am, that's all I know." He smiles with a bewildered charm designed to cut inquiry short. "Do you want it or not?"

"Sure," Lili says. It would be bad luck to put things back, though the avocados look overripe and she has no respect for canned garbanzos. Among the foodstuffs, after all, lie a pair of ugly, cocoa-plaid shoelaces and a Teflon scrubber for pots and pans. Lili studies the architecture of half a red cabbage. This "ma'am-ing" has cropped up the past year or so as her graying hair inches its way to silver. The young man, though Hispanic, bears an astonishing resemblance to Danny Welles, an old classmate of hers in Terre Haute who burned the junior high down the summer after seventh grade and went away to military school. Like everyone else, Lili called him "Torch" behind his back, and she suffers a fleeting remorse now as she counts bills into the palm of this slender, heavy-lidded boy. In crowds, Lili's a person people choose to ask what time it is. At home, unloading bags from car to curb, she's appalled by her own absurdity.

Lili eats tortillas with Muenster for days while the Praise-a-thon continues on channel 40. *Roll of carpet in center lane, causing a bit of a swerve.* The Learning Channel has safety instruction (never, ever dart from between parked cars). There's a warning that acrylic nails can make your own fall off, and yogurt may cause ovarian cancer. Africanized killer bees are oozing their way toward California, and the ozone in smog can weaken condoms to the point of failure. (She ought to drop Garrett a note about this, not that she has his address.) Support groups appear on talk shows to confess the devastation of winning lotteries. Lili is heating her tortillas right on the gas flame, shaving the cheese so thin that it melts on contact. What can be meant by *Africanized?* Perhaps she has misunderstood everything.

The phone jars, slicing straight through her chest. She is short of breath and clammy by the time she picks it up, though she knows it can't be him. He won't call before the thing is over, and obviously it's too soon for that. Rhea pretends she's confirming the date of Lili's scheduled return to work, but more likely word of the split is out and she's calling to monitor damage so she can update the staff. "I wasn't sure I'd catch you at home," she says. "I thought you were heading up the coast."

Indeed, Lili told this preposterous lie. "Not yet," she says now. "Not for a day or two at least."

"Well, that sounds wonderful," Rhea says. "It just sounds perfectly wonderful."

"Doesn't it?" Lili responds evenly.

"So how are you?" Rhea wants to know.

"Fine," Lili purrs. "And how are you?"

"Listen, if you're having ill effects from the collision, you ought to sneak in here and let Ted shoot some cervicals. Are you sure you want to use up both your weeks at once? You know what chaos we plunge into here when you're gone."

Lili manages to emit the proper cheery noises, then catches the second half of *Murder by Television*, a Bela Lugosi thriller from 1935 in which cameras turn into actual death rays.

It's late and Lili's amusing herself with a tumbler of gin in the bathroom. She has been making faces in the mirror but now sits on a redwood stool by the tub watching tiny ants scurry busily up and down the porcelain to no discernible purpose. Casually, precisely, she bears down on one with the edge of her glass. Demolished, it becomes the sudden focus of its fellows who, within moments, organize themselves as pallbearers and tote the remains back into the tile crack that must lead to their nest. Who would imagine ants to be so decent, though for all she knows they may devour, not bury, the thing in the dark. At Thrifty's this afternoon the cosmetic computer recommended Natural Ivory Translucent Powder for her day shade, Ivory Bisque for evening wear. It demanded to know whether her skin coloring was ivory or pale, pinkish ivory, golden peachy ivory, or sallow. Lili punched SALLOW at first to see what would happen, but sickly yellow proved to be of no consequence at all with the proper Concealer and Natural Finish. She was strongly advised to purchase from the warm, vital tones displayed in Color Group Four.

Reaching for aspirin she's confronted with Garrett's thick white shaving mug, a short-lived phase he went through a few months before, banishing throwaway plastic and cans of foam. His old-fashioned, double-edge steel razor lies behind the cup, next to an ivory-handled brush. Lili downs three tablets, smears Plum Storm over dry but tingly lips and debates whether she can safely shave her legs. She sips gin and stares at the vivid imprint her mouth leaves, as if the glass belongs not to her but some cheap and emphatic stranger. There are loose blades scattered over the topmost shelf, and Lili begins to drop them, one by one, into the narrow disposal slot at the back of the medicine cabinet. They make no sound as they disappear, and she is mystified about where they go—into a hollow wall, perhaps, or two floors down to the basement, where they pile up to pose one of life's concealed threats.

Pants rolled high, Lili perches on the rim of the tub and ignores the ants, loading the razor, enjoying its heft. The yellowed soap at the bottom of the mug yields a surprising and luxuriant menthol lather, which she brushes slowly over her calves. GUARANTEED 100% BOAR BRISTLE, the handle proclaims—so the superior hairs of uncastrated male pigs play this valuable role in the removal of men's beards. There is always some kind of beauty to logic. Ahead of her in the drugstore line stood a very muscular, acne-scarred young man whose Beastie Boys T-shirt said GET OFF MY DICK. In Garrett's toiletry drawer she discovered only a Ziploc plastic bagful of soap ends, which he liked to save, soak, and mash together into "new" bars, an unappealing habit Lili grew accustomed to over the years, finally found endearing in a way. Garrett must have pictured himself unpacking a year's worth of old soap slivers in front of Penny, which would not do at all—better start fresh and break the child in gradually. And yet he lacked the gallantry to throw this prize collection away. Lili rinses lather and hair down the drain, then uses tweezers to scrape moist shards of soapcake from the cup into the plastic bag.

Over the weekend in Vegas a man was struck by lightning as he rode on the back of a motorcycle, although the woman driving was reportedly unfazed. Lili has stripped and finally crawled into bed, switching from call-in radio to Dr. Gene Scott on channel 30, or rather, to his empty chair, for Scott has carried out last night's threat to abandon his viewers if they didn't reach the pledge goal of $246,000 by showtime. Lili has become a reluctant fan of this rotund and white-haired preacher who tries to prove he's not a television evangelist by wearing raffish hats and sunglasses, smoking cigars, cussing, and picking his nose in constant close-up. Intelligence and wit and biblical scholarship very nearly camouflage the megalomania, though he does declare that when people are devastated by circumstance, the devil always puts them out of his broadcast range. "If you are devastated by a circumstance, you know what to do? Sell your car and buy a dish, go rent a cheap room and sit there and watch me till your sanity comes back. Now get on the telephone. The Lord loves a cheerful giver." Even his empty, overstuffed chair is supposed to be worthy of attention as phone numbers roll across the bottom of the screen in silence, devoid of the usual Merle Haggard or Pointer Sisters tapes. Lili stares and stares, fascinated by the pull of this theatrical hostility. The tension is unbearable, and yet one bears it. One bears it because one expects the old goat to reappear any second. As soon as she realizes this, Lili gets up to unplug the set and roll it back among shadows in the living room.

Full moonlight draws her to the tallest French window, a warm, dry breeze caressing her breasts. She can see into the building out back, complete but as yet unoccupied. For days the force of compressors has rattled dishes up and down the block, spraying stucco everywhere, including Lili's windowpanes. Yesterday a detail crew returned, one *compadre* calling "holiday, holiday" and pointing, another aiming his hose to fill the crevices. Lili studies the backside of an unconnected stove, its bulky presence emphasizing hollow spaces through dark glass. She's aroused that she could be seen here, pale and trembling and in clear view, if anyone was there to look. Through a vacant doorway behind the stove, just at the top of an angled staircase, there might be a man who watches her. She can almost make him out in silhouette, though he dares not move or speak. Lili sways and opens herself in silver light, releasing quick and sharp to emptiness.

Lately the car is stifling, even with the windows down. She is determined, finally, to deposit Garrett's check for his half of two months' rent, intended to provide Lili time to find herself a smaller place. She can't seem to manage the ignition key this morning, though, suddenly convinced she's let the brake work go too long. She pictures a dense line of signals along the obstacle course to the bank and realizes she will have to walk. Fortunately, after the remnants of last night's oatmeal and a small pitcher of modified screwdrivers, she has extracted her ancient white Tretorns from way back in the closet, from way back before Garrett, when she toyed with tennis, and she has spruced them up with the atrocious laces destined hers from the grocery store. *It's a game of hopscotch on the Hollywood North.* She has ruined her best green belt trying to punch an extra hole with a paring knife.

Wells Fargo is so eerily quiet, without a soul in line, that Lili checks immediately for a robbery in progress. On the security screen she monitors herself along the cordoned pathway to the tellers until out of nowhere a very high–heeled woman deftly steps over the rope in front of her.

"Excuse me," Lili says, before she can click ahead to the one open window. "I think I was here first, if you don't mind."

"NO YOU WEREN'T," the woman rasps, loud enough to make the guard step forward to investigate. "I WAS HERE FIRST. HOW ELSE COULD I BE IN FRONT OF YOU? GOD." This lady is dressed with powerful elegance, fashionably layered, precisely made up, and Lili is frightened by her well harnessed breasts and glossy, deep red nails.

"You stepped over the rope," she offers meekly, just audible through pounding blood in her neck.

"IT DOESN'T MATTER HOW YOU GET HERE. WE CAME AT THE SAME TIME." Now all personnel are on alert.

"I don't think so," Lili says. "What do you think the rope is for?"

"Oh, go ahead." The woman has switched to a nasty croon, motioning her by as if she were a child, though Lili's her senior by at least ten years. "Go ahead, go ahead. You can go ahead. It's obviously very important to you."

"Fine," Lili says. "I will go ahead. But it wasn't so important to me that I cut in line." A second teller wisely opens up, and the women stand side by side for their transactions, amid a kind of electrical perfume. Lili is shaken and drained, humiliated in spite of being right, inflamed enough to envision knocking this gal down and stomping her face.

She considers a bus back up Western but has no change and is unsure of routes. Instead she zigzags her way to Serrano and trudges over the hill, past a block of dilapidated bungalow courts, nestled with clusters of tall, dying palms. On one of the tiny porches sits an extraordinarily obese young Caucasian in a sleeveless dress, a plastic jug of water in her lap.

"Look at the fake jogger," she glares at Lili. "Look at that skinny-ass narc who thinks we sell cocaine. Well, we don't. And you better quit going by here. I see you go by here fifteen times a day. You think it's a secret? You think you're undercover? You must think you're watching everybody and nobody's watching you. That's how stupid you are."

Lili cannot fall asleep but has sunk into a reverie of mattresses. Doubles and singles, fulls and twins, kings and queens. Nowadays they're covered with something glossy, colorful, resistant to stain. She should go directly to a warehouse, haul home a narrow ultrafirm and lay it flat out on the floor, though some still swear by waterbeds. Lili has never slept in a bunk but imagines herself a stupid radio psychologist, recommending them for sagging marriages. "Confide like children at summer camp. Take absolutely nothing for granted. Flip a coin for who's on top." She is stretched along the diagonal, which ought to but doesn't absorb Garrett's space. The lure of motels and everything we hope not to smell there. In high school she wore short-shorts made of ticking.

Flashes of pale pink light mean Yolanda next door is sneaking out again. This scenario has been playing since last Sunday night—Good Girl Blown Off Course by Santa Ana Winds. Lili's got the routine down pat and no longer bothers to get up and peek. Around ten o'clock Yolanda's suitor brings her home, or at least to the curb in front of her home, where they sit in his shiny, low-riding Buick and make out ferociously until Mr. Lopez calls his daughter to the porch. Yolanda sidles past him, on inside, where both parents berate her loudly in Spanish until they exhaust themselves and darken the house. An hour or so later the Christmas lights, strung for keeps around the edge of the roof, begin to blink erratically, as if a child were playing with the plug. Soon the screen door clicks open and Yolanda tiptoes out, clutching shoes like a doll against her breast. The Buick coasts down the hill without lights, losing momentum by the time it arrives so that both kids have to push till they can gun the motor beyond the yard. Late summer winds full of dry excitement bring on this yearning for danger and hard, moist heat. Lili feels past risking everything for sex, though her relief at this is tarnished by nostalgia and her envy of Garrett. Fires have been raging and smoldering in Griffith Park all week. The breeze picks up just enough to loosen one dead frond from the palm across the street—Lili hears it separate and hit the pavement, stem first, with an unmistakable twangy *thud*. It will lie there at the edge of the gutter for cars to avoid as they slow for turns.

Lili is making a list, for unless she topples into sick leave, she must return to the clinic on Monday. BRAKES, she writes, and BODY WORK. CLEAN OUT FRIDGE. LOOK FOR APARTMENT. She hesitates, then surprises herself with LOOK FOR JOB, though she adds an immediate question mark, resenting this veer from dismay into melodrama *(motor home ablaze in the carpool lane)*. Neverthelsss she retrieves a Sunday paper from the bottom of the corner pile and browses her way through classified employment. Front office gigs nearly always demand light typing, communication skills, and a "pleasant, efficient personality," if not a downright "sunny disposition." The Performing Arts Radiology Center insists as well on "ability to interact w/famous entertainment clientele."

Someone is "Desperately Seeking Manicurists," and "Telephone Actresses" are in very great demand ("Adult Party Line from home or office. All shifts open. Must be outgoing and have a good imagination. Bilingual a plus.") Lili could move her phone from the hallway closet, set up office right in bed, re-create herself as extrovert, learn the Spanish word for *suck*. She dials the B. Hills ad for "Live-in Laundress" and hangs up twice on a male British accent. She's been following reruns of *The Singing Detective* and nursing a bit of a crush on his wife. She adds WASH CURTAINS to her list of otherwise unlikely goals.

An old-fashioned, single-level department store on Larchmont makes Lili feel like Indiana, and of late she is partial to notions and sundries, having purchased on sale not only three clear plastic rain bonnets in carrying cases, one iridescent Virgo key chain, and two fat burgundy penlights, but also a small brown pair of binoculars, actually a flask. She unscrews both lenses now and pours gin with lime for the laundromat, though none of the items was purchased with intent. Dragging her canvas bagful of curtains and sheets down the sidewalk, fake opera glasses strapped inelegantly about her neck, Lili achieves an exquisite silliness for herself, enhanced when she comes upon a curbside shopping cart, transfers her load and picks up speed. Outside the Wash House another shopping cart is parked, this one loaded down with bags of clothing and trash, its distinctive feature being two tan Chihuahuas hung over the side in padded, red cotton harnesses. The dogs are ancient and appear content, supported from the bottom, backs against wire, front paws exposed like babies' arms. On the concrete beneath them sit two tiny dishes of food and water, encircled precisely by short, thin leashes. Their keeper—fat and filthy and fervently psychotic—is inside doing her version of laundry, a débâcle that Lili has witnessed before.

Garrett's white briefs turn up again, having been dropped into this bag last time when she balked at putting them away. She will throw them in with the kitchen curtains to balance out a load. At the far end of the premises the dog woman keeps shouting, "There's a balm in Gilead," over and over until Lili recognizes the anthem she sang in Girl Scout chorus, under the fierce direction of Miss Veronica Hussong. She is ready for a taste of gimlet but cannot bring herself to drink from the binoculars, peering through them instead at wild, chartreuse distortions—a disembodied soap dispenser floats right toward her face. For a quarter she could gain admittance to the restroom, but guzzling in the toilet strikes her ludicrous as well. She sits down with a crossword from the *Times,* immediately confirmed in that giraffes were once *camelopards.* A tall, exceedingly narrow black man begins to fidget and pace in front of her, flipping up his washer lid every few minutes, in such a hurry he slows down each cycle. His impatience is catching, and Lili's tired of waiting, too, for things to run their own sweet course.

The trick is to fetch curtains from the dryer before the crumpling gets baked in. She fears she may have missed the moment but hopes that gravity will work on the rods. She folds the panels quickly in half and arranges them neatly across her cart. Outside she pauses to pet the Chihuahuas, slipping the flask around one's neck, to hilarious effect, then depositing the thing among the madwoman's bags.

"I wasn't simply pinned to the boy, dear daughter," a woman passing by informs her bored and spike-haired teenage companion. "At the time we were actually already lavaliered."

In the dream a librarian marks her past due. Lili has collected a fearsome array of small tin clips discarded from the County Museum and hopes thereby to save the price of admission, though when she arrives, third Tuesdays are free. She sits on the floor cross-legged beneath a Schiele townscape until an undulating crowd appears to block it out. No one looks at the nudes next door, but Lili's coerced onto some stairs that curve through the cafeteria, where it feels like everyone's birthday. She can't make them understand the gravel in her shoes or that she has lost her library card. "My husband's on helium," she insists, as if this were the missing link. The walls seem to vibrate with fading Polaroids.

Lili has cleaned up her act with the gin and finally feels like reading but lacks the right text. She skims through a best-selling thriller, discovered on a linen shelf, but can't quite care who kills whom or why. Murder mysteries pale against the real ones. How, for example, did this brand-new, twenty-dollar hardback book she has never seen or heard of wind up inside her most private of closets? Not something Garrett would buy, she's sure, though life's little certainties do erode. The mystery of murder is not who does it so much as how it might feel. She would like to shoot the cycle boys who keep racing motors beneath her window, then peeling out around the corner. She will perch with a rifle against the screen and pick them off as they zoom up the hill. Become a devoted jailhouse lawyer, best career move she could make. Rhea forever carries forty extra pounds but is always poised to begin reform. There will be halfway amusing gibes tomorrow at Lili's increased angularity.

Since early morning, through a series of catnaps, she has been wondering about a boy from her high school paper, the boy who took her to their graduation dance. There was nothing strange in the date itself, though Ken was shy and eccentric and it had been their only one. Around 5:00 A.M. his parents, in a full-size, overloaded U-Haul, came rumbling into the lakeside lot where diehard seniors still partied in cars. Ken had not mentioned a move to Chicago, but soon he was off with his dad in the truck, his mom close behind in the station wagon, Lili left to hitch a ride for breakfast at the Wagon Wheel. Halfway through his journalism major Ken broke down into someone who couldn't think or bathe or wear any shoes, though he stabilized enough later on to carry a neighborhood paper route. Years after she divorced and moved west, Ken called her parents' house and said, "Tell Lili hi and I'm still with the *Trib*." She can see his face more clearly now than that of the boy she married at twenty, surely part of what it means to age, the way things start to sort themselves.

She almost doesn't answer Garrett's knock, certain it's Testigos de Jehovah. Without glasses he looks exhausted and fully fifty, peering over two brown bags of groceries. The sight of him is slightly dizzying, but Lili doesn't flinch.

"Did you come for your underwear?" she says. "It's immaculate. Truly. Beyond white all the way to bright. Did you leave a book in the bathroom closet? What's all this food?"

"I thought you might let me fix something," Garrett says, not stepping in until she motions.

"Fix something here? Is something broken?"

"I thought I might fix salmon," he says, ignoring the words, keying only to her undertone of yes.

"Go in the kitchen," Lili says. She ducks into the

bathroom and shuts the door, steadying herself against the sink, running cold water over her wrists, emphatically avoiding lipstick.

"I saw the car," Garrett says as she makes her entrance. "I heard you got creamed but not hurt. Rhea said you had gone up the coast."

"Do I look like I've been up the coast, Garrett? Do I look to you like a woman who's been vacationing up the coast?" He looks at her but doesn't answer. "What were you doing down in X ray, anyway? I thought you were strictly into Personnel these days. So to speak."

He is sitting very still at the table, not in his usual place. "She doesn't know anything about anything," he finally says, barely above a whisper.

"Really." She can't resist. "Somehow I thought that was the point."

"Would you mind if I open this wine?" Garrett says, reaching for a sack. He will be a guest until she touches him, which isn't yet.

"Of course I realize how tiresome I must be, knowing absolutely everything the way I do," she says.

"It wouldn't hurt if you blinked once in a while," Garrett agrees, pouring Chablis. "Avert your gaze, just momentarily. Believe me, it would be a relief to all concerned. Give those baby blues a rest."

"It wouldn't hurt if you opened yours up once in a while, either," Lili says, not angrily. "Take a good hard look around just once."

"Let's drink to it," he says. They raise the glasses separately.

"Where are your spectacles?" Lili asks.

"Somebody stepped on them," he says, and she stares at him till she can see it was Penny.

"Jesus," she laughs.

"You did the curtains." Garrett lets out a deliberate snort at the grossly wrinkled hanging mess. "I'll have to bring the iron in and go over them, for what it's worth."

So everything is with him in the car. Lili pretends to scrutinize the fish, pretends almost to turn up her nose. "I've got a jicama," she says, shockingly enthusiastic.

"You've got a what?"

"I've got a jicama. Do you know what it is? Neither do I. Let's eat some and see. What do you think?"

"I think we might ought to get married," Garrett says.

"That's possibly the most ridiculous statement you ever uttered in your life," Lili says from the fridge. "Don't you wonder where I got this thing? I've developed a whole new shopping technique. The freezer is jammed with pork chops and tortillas."

Garrett sits quietly, sipping his wine, as Lili rises to the surface where it's possible to breathe.

Los Angeles
Here and Now

Mid-morning the ashes of her neighbor's son arrive still warm from somewhere in the Valley. The boy who delivers them may or may not realize the nature of his cargo, having no command of English and appearing to expect a tip. He offers no receipt to sign, and Fran doesn't bother to steer him next door, simply transferring the blond, fake wood case directly from his hands onto the red canvas chair inside her narrow hallway. She knows that Carol is off to a doctor in search of a drug that will make her stop weeping.

Carol hasn't lived here long, having moved in from the beach to take an office job downtown (in from the beach and away from Joey). At twenty-two the boy was still an ardent surfer, much too adept, even at riptide, to snap his neck and drown, though this is what he did. Fran has seen pictures of Joey at every age on his mother's walls but never actually met him, which complicates her feelings now as she clears off the small oak table in her breakfast nook and carefully centers the tepid box, less with sadness than a cloying sense of awe. She hears a starched and solemn voice from her grandfather's funeral years ago: *We brought nothing into this world, and it is certain we can carry nothing out.*

Fran and Carol are the same age and friendly, take in an occasional movie together, toured the Frank Lloyd Wright house at Barnsdall Park one extra-smoggy Sunday afternoon. They keep track of neighborhood graffiti and gunshots and abandoned cars and share lists of toll-free numbers for futile complaints to the city. Carol has always talked more about Joey than about herself, a habit that has intensified in the week since his death. There is never a mention of the father, and Fran has run out of impotent, comforting words. She moves to the sink to wash her hands and stares at a framed lunar postcard of Earth. Fran spent the first moon landing (her first honeymoon) making love on the floor of an empty house, empty, that is, but for TV and mattress. For years she viewed the famous photos through that fleshy, myopic memory, though of late the blue-black image has widened, beyond the whirl of days and months.

She should be at work, but it gusted rain all night and drowned her car, soaking wires past any hope of ignition. Nate at Old Volks advised her to remove the distributor cap and blow on the connectors, which Fran has done, plus wiped everything with paper towel. She put a garbage bag over the engine, beneath the stupidly vented hood, and has come upstairs to wait for evaporation. On this first day of mandatory rationing, well into a five-year drought, water has burst through her living room ceiling. She's been half watching a talk show on osteoporosis, trying not to hear the drips in the bucket, but now she turns the TV off to listen for the click of Carol's key next door. Once it comes, she waits a bit before calling.

"Carol?" she says. "Listen. There was a delivery while you were gone."

"A delivery?" Carol says vaguely.

"From the Valley," Fran says.

"Oh, God," Carol says. "They told me afternoon. Not before three."

"Yes, I think they were supposed to wait," Fran says, unable, quite, to mention temperature. "But anyway, I'll be right there."

As it happens, once over the tactile shock—Fran sees it register in her weary gray eyes and thin twist of mouth—Carol seems to take comfort in the heat, snuggling up to the tin-lined box as she curls herself onto the couch.

"Do you want me to call your brother?" Fran asks. "Maybe your sister-in-law can come and stay a couple more nights."

"They're back in Vegas now," Carol says. "They've got problems of their own."

"Well. Do you want anything before I go?" Fran eyes what looks like half a pound of pale blue oval tablets spread out on the hardwood floor.

"I took two and spilled the rest," Carol explains, both hands on the box against her belly. She is a lanky woman, the palest kind of blonde, her skin translucent now with days of grief.

"Where did you find this doctor?" Fran asks.

"West Hollywood," Carol says. "He was really nice. He said this is the worst thing that can happen to a person, to lose a child. He went ahead and wrote refills, too."

"Hmm," Fran says, bending to scoop the pills back into their bottle. "I'm going to put these in the bathroom. I'm going to put them inside your medicine chest. Then I'm going on to work if the car will start. And check back with you when I get home." Carol responds to none of this, so Fran lets herself out, locking the knob.

Traffic is jammed and detoured onto Beverly due to a fallen palm across Wilton, but nobody's honking. Pedestrians seem frisky in the rain, parched souls sprung to life like those flattened sponges. Fran's engine dies at every light but reignites with little strain. At Crenshaw and Venice she pulls up behind a tiny, white-haired lady wearing gossamer wings that project higher than the car seat, higher even than her head. Her bouffant appears to float back and forth in time with her windshield wipers, and as she leans forward to execute her turn, she makes ascension look accessible. Fran considers skipping the workday afternoon to follow this battered green Mercury wherever it might lead. She sees herself slipping into the rear pew of a white frame church, privy to a winged pageant. *Cremains* is the word for what's in the box, a word Fran has seen in print before, surely a mortician's word and not a word that people speak. *Cremains*. Her eyes fill up over this word, obviously devised to squelch emotion. Some weeks ago in a grocery store she quietly burst into tears when a man accused his wife of being on the rag. Early menopause is warping her nerves toward some eccentric clarity. On the radio Van Morrison still believes it's a marvelous night for a moondance, is begging to make some more romance.

"No," Fran thinks. "No more romance. Thank you very much." She's been alone since Kathryn, nearly two years, and feels like a wise old virgin, as wary of woman's determination to merge as of men's determination not to.

On the porch of the shelter Capricia stands waiting, a cigarette in each hand. "You late, Miss Fannie May," she says. "You get you butt fired like that. That's what they tell me. You the secatary, you got to be here don't mean maybe."

"I couldn't help it," Fran says. "I was at the mercy of the rain. Or at the mercy of my distributor cap."

Capricia tosses both smokes into the waterlogged bushes that frame the sidewalk and follows Fran inside. To stay at the shelter the residents have to see a psychiatrist but by law can't be forced to take the meds he prescribes. Capricia's paranoia has been on the rise, and with it her rambunctiousness, so Fran is hoping not to get cornered alone in the downstairs office.

"At the mercy of that distributing cap," Capricia says. "I heard that. I'm at the mercy of dogshit." Fran keys into the familiar undertone of rage that keeps her from laughing at this and does not invite elaboration. "Every time I go to McDonald's some big ol' dog is out there in the parking lot taking a shit, and people start to laugh at me. Every damn time." Capricia pauses to watch Fran lock her purse away in the filing cabinet. "I'm sick of it, too." Her voice rises in pain. "They look at that dogshit, and then they look at me and laugh. Don't tell me they don't."

Fran doesn't doubt that people might be laughing at Capricia, who at five-three weighs well over two hundred pounds and wears bulge-hugging elastic skirts above her knees. "Maybe they're laughing at something else," Fran says. "You never know what people are laughing at. It doesn't have to be at you, just because you see them laughing."

"They laughin' at me all right. And that damn ol' dog follows me to these restaurants so they can humiliate me. It's very precise, believe me. It's not some accidental recurring dream, or whatever you want to call it. It's all to the purpose, but I don't know what the purpose is. I'd like just once to be left alone."

"Well, I'll leave you alone," Fran says. "I've got charts to xerox upstairs."

"They say to let your little light shine, though," Capricia advises. "Might be somebody down in the valley tryin' to get home."

"I drove in behind an angel," Fran tells her from the steps. "I mean, a little lady was wearing wings and driving."

"M-hm," Capricia says. "I heard that. I heard that one, but good."

"Come on up later if you want me to help you go through the closet and look for a longer skirt," Fran says. "There could be something in there that would fit."

"I don't want no long skirt," Capricia says.

"Remember Dr. Berman suggested you find something more appropriate to wear?" Fran issues this reminder as gently as possible. "He thought you might feel better in something more modest. You might not get hassled so much on the street. You know what I'm talking about."

"He's tellin' me what to wear and him wearin' that skullcap," Capricia says. When she laughs her eyes shut tight while her mouth expands to astounding width. "He got it so far back on his head he have to wear bobby pins to keep it from fallin' off. But Jesus said the circumcision wouldn't do them any good. He sendeth rain on the just and the unjust alike, and that include Mr. Get-Back-Honky-Cat George Heebie-Jeebie Bush."

"Well, let me know if you change your mind," Fran says. "Or I can give you a note for the thrift shop."

"You go with me, I'll go," Capricia says. "I done told you that yesterday."

"I can't go with you," Fran says. "One of the counselors can go with you. Dennis can go with you."

"He laughs out both sides of his mouth," Capricia says. "If he thinks he's on a pedestal, he ought to think again. It's all he can do to keep from pullin' his dick out every time he sees me, anyway. Let him that thinketh he standeth take heed lest he fall."

"I wish you'd give the Haldol another try," Fran says.

"You try it, I'll try it," Capricia says. "See how you like it for a change. The only thing drivin' me crazy is this dogshit business. Ain't no medicine about to fix that."

"It might," Fran says. "It might make things seem different to you."

"So would her-oin," Capricia says. "And be a lot more fun, too." She pulls a pack of Eve cigarettes from a pocket tight beneath her armpit and turns toward the exit. "If He shall give thee the desires of thy heart, then it means He'll give me you. The rain has no father and it has no mother, and neither do I." She closes the door softly behind her.

"How's your girlfriend?" Dennis is grinning his handsome young grin at the top of the stairs. "If you'll go to the bathroom, I'll go to the bathroom."

"It's charming the way you amuse yourself," Fran says

dryly, grabbing his chiseled upper arm. "Maybe someday you'll amuse others, too."

By four the rain has slowed to mist, and on her way home Fran pulls into Ralph's, as close to the exit as she can get. People often toss receipts into the trash bin there, and on the back of some of these are coupons for free frozen yogurt at the mini–mall across the street. She lifts an address book from her purse and uses it to fan herself. So far she can discern no pattern in what sets off the flashes of heat. Having to call the car shop seemed to do it, and having to change the Xerox toner. The thought of Joey's ashes has brought on more than one today, along with the image of being smothered in Capricia's mass of flesh. At night it may be dreams, though when she wakes up with the burning that turns to cold sweat, it feels merely thermal, untied to sex or the usual terrors. Most likely the heat flares up in cycles, controlled by hormones rather than life. She's as weird as Capricia, determined to fix a causal link between defecating dogs and random laughter. In any case, the weather has helped, but still Fran is craving something cold. A young woman with an infant strapped to her belly unloads a basket two cars down and doesn't bother to retrieve the curled receipt that rolls out from one bag. Fran waits a discreet amount of time before she lifts the thing from a shallow puddle.

The tiny shop is deserted except for the somber, teenaged Korean in charge, who quickly serves Fran and silently accepts the soggy ticket, then resumes her seat at the table up front and continues to read her Bible, printed in vertical rows of delicate black. The whole side wall is mirror, and Fran chooses the only spot in the place where she won't be forced to watch herself eat. The creamy chocolate and toffee yogurt soothes the back of her head and chills the base of her throat, where fire concentrates at times. These vivid flavors neutralize the shelter odor on her clothes, a faint combination of smoke and must. Somewhere in her daze of pleasure she becomes aware that the cashier has cozied up to the mirror, examining zits. Fran watches, incredulous, as the young lady begins to squeeze her chin, not once, not twice, but on and on, even as Fran walks past and out the door. She's been scavenging freebies for weeks now at two bucks a slap, and here's retribution (from a girl at the mercy of hormones herself). Fran finishes her treat in the car with the radio up. Astonishingly, Bob Dylan is turning fifty, and some phony DJ wag is playing "Knockin' on Heaven's Door" in honor of his birthday and "Hard Rain" in honor of precipitation.

Her mailbox is so stuffed with junk mail that Fran tears the cover off *Newsweek* getting it out. Once for an old friend's birthday she ordered a Thomas Merton tape, so she's been slotted into numerous religious and New Age mailing lists. She is now invited to purchase subliminal cassettes of magical affirmations (*My mindpower rejuvenates me. My body remolds into perfection. My mental abilities*

sharpen with the years. I am a powerhouse of boundless energy.)
Deep weariness settles behind Fran's knees as she reads
and climbs the steps into her building. There are two
identical bright blue envelopes from Servants of the Par-
aclete requesting that she send fifty dollars to relieve
the poignant plight of priests who suffer spiritual emptiness. Fran might, if she had the cash, send twenty-five
to the Union of Global Women to eradicate
clitoridectomies.

She dials Carol's number before stretching out for a
nap. "So how's it been?" she says.

"At least I'm not crying," Carol answers hoarsely, over-
enunciating through the drug. "There was a moment
when I could almost believe what's happened, but it
passed. I'm afraid if I take down my garbage, somebody
will break in here and steal him."

"I'll take it out later," Fran says. "I'll come over and
see what needs doing." A pause elongates the space between them. "A mourning dove has built a nest in the
signal on Serrano," she offers. "It blocks the whole green
light when the bird is there."

"I have to lie back down," Carol says, "before sunlight
starts hitting this bed and throwing shadows on my
mirror. Lately that really gives me the creeps."

It is nearly eight when Fran taps next door for garbage, taking her own down as well, having to pour water
off the flat barrel lids out back. Another storm is gather-

ing, due in before midnight. She carefully redrapes her VW engine in plastic. Carol's apartment is still dark behind her when she answers the door again, though she's semi-dressed and Fran smells burnt toast. Carol clicks on the muted hallway bulb, then leads Fran to the living room and fumbles for lamplight. She is wearing a pale green cotton robe with jeans on underneath. The low lilt of a radio drifts in from the bedroom on heavy air, and in one corner the unlovely blond box occupies a stuffed chair, the comfortable chair, beneath a long-chained bamboo swag light. The women settle on the couch, not quite facing each other.

"More rain," Fran says. "The sound is so soothing. Except in my living room, where it's a drip at a time."

"I hope it stays cloudy," Carol says. "I couldn't bear a sunny, blue-sky day right now. I hope it clouds over for a month."

"Ever hear Willie Nelson sing 'Blue Skies'?" Fran asks. "The words are happy, but he sings it so slow, it wrings you out." She accompanies herself on imaginary guitar. "Blooooooo skiiiiiiiiiiiies, smiiiiiiiiiilin' at me, nothin' but blooooooo skiiiiiiiiiies do I see. Deer-neer-neer." Carol reaches into a pocket for Kleenex, sinking Fran's heart. "God, I'm sorry," she says.

Carol waves this off but sniffles on for a while before getting up. "I'm past time for a pill is all," she says. "Please stay till it kicks in. Sing me something else."

"I guess I won't sing," Fran says. While Carol is in

the bathroom the Beach Boys glide through on the radio. She snaps them off on her way back in.

"I never wanted him on the boards," she says. "I worried myself sick all the way through his childhood, but there we were, and there seemed to be no stopping him, the way he loved the water. Quite obviously I should have stopped him. I should have never let it get started in the first place. So now here we are." She looks toward the shadowed corner, but her face doesn't break.

"You mustn't think about it that way," Fran says softly. "He could as easily have been taken doing something else. It was his life to live."

"His life to live and his death to die," Carol says with an edge. "I can't believe he would leave me like this."

The moment grows long and silent except for the hollow sound of slow rain hitting palm fronds. Fran has heard suicide called the ultimate declaration of independence, and maybe any death is that. Fran can't imagine either having a child or losing one. She feels herself blush with heat and shifts on the sofa, takes a deep breath as if that will help. She thinks of mentioning the driving angel but decides against it. In *Wings of Desire* there were all those beautiful male angels in business suits, hovering in the library.

Carol picks up the remote control and begins pushing buttons. Flooded streets in Van Nuys cut to fire in San Francisco, cars in pursuit, a couple in bed. "Joey calls this channel surfing."

"Clever," Fran says, uneasy with the tense, which

Carol lets stand without a blink. Fran feels a perfect circle of sweat break out around the crown of her head. *Fontanelle*, they called it, in her baby-sitting days, the soft spot. What yarmulkes cover up. Carol finally lands for a moment on Marlon Brando, defending his bail-freed son in a most humble voice. His loose black raincoat makes him much, much fatter than surely he can be. Fran remembers him not so much in the T-shirt in *Streetcar* as in the camel coat in *Tango*, putting it to Maria Schneider standing up. It is painful now to look at him, the way his body's become such a burden.

Carol flips to PBS, which is rerunning Bill Moyers on "Amazing Grace." *'Tis grace that brought me safe thus far, and grace will take me home.*

"Oh, puh-lease," Carol nearly shouts at the screen. Her eyelids are pulled unnaturally wide, and it occurs to Fran that she has popped the wrong pill or too much of the right one or maybe something else altogether. She stands up and surfs from 28 to 56 with several audible intakes of breath, rhythmically waving the remote at arm's length as if to keep her balance. "Here we are, here we are," she says. "This shopping thing. They talk until you're hypnotized, and then they toot a little horn to break the spell." Gingerly she lays the remote on the glass coffee table and arranges herself back on the couch. "Feet up," she tells Fran. "We can both fit our feet up if we work it right." Her robe has slipped sideways so that one breast is nearly exposed, a dishevelment startling in a woman prone to turtlenecks and three-piece office suits. "Because this is the only show that won't make it worse," she adds, as if Fran had asked for an explanation.

A perky organ rendition of "California Dreamin' " reminds Fran that she never learned to skate, while a gaudy piece of jewelry spins slowly in the center of the screen. An overly enthused male voice announces that this is a Cubic Zirconia Diamond Spectacular Pendant, which retails for 299.95. At the moment, however, it's a CZ Special, running not at $150, not at 140 and not at 130. Not even at 119.95, but at $99. "No," he says. "Tell you what. We're going to let you have it for $74.25. No, wait, ladies and gentlemen. Can you believe this? We'll run it for eight minutes only at the incredible price of 29.75. Look at that. As that pendant revolves around and catches the light, you can perceive its heavenly beauty."

The weariness is back, behind Fran's knees. Her nap after work was an anxious one with an outlandish dream involving stolen shoes, a black Ferris wheel, and flammable cotton candy vomit.

"See?" Carol says. "What did I tell you? Isn't this amazing?"

"It is amazing," Fran says. Her right calf feels seared where it's been touching Carol's, and the heat now shoots up her thigh, then up her spine and into the base of her throat. "If you're feeling steady for a while, I think I'll go on home," she says, but before Carol can respond there's a sudden banging next door.

It's a long gaze through the peephole before Fran lets register the fact that Capricia is standing patiently in the corridor with a very long-stemmed bird-of-paradise tucked beneath one arm. If Fran could get away with it, she might retreat on tiptoe and try to ignore the knocking. Her experience with Capricia, however, has been that she's not a woman easily ignored.

"Just a minute," she calls through the door. "I'll be out in a minute. Just hold on." Quickly, and without consulting Carol on the couch, Fran dials the shelter for Bayne, the evening counselor. "Capricia Laidlaw is knocking at my door right now," she tells him. "What the hell is going on?"

"She's been discharged," Bayne says. "That's all I know. Dennis found her in the office before shift change, going through the Rolodex. Maybe she got your address out of there. She threw the thing at him on her way out, along with a few choice words. He smelled booze on her, too. You know she's been pushing limits all week and riling all the women up. So she finally managed to get herself kicked out."

"Well, can somebody come and get her?" Fran says. "She can just as well set off again in the morning if she'll go back."

"Nobody here but us chickens," Bayne says. "I mean, this chicken. I'm the only chicken here because Gary called in sick. Dennis gave Capricia bus tokens to get to the Sundown Mission, anyway."

"Wonderful, Bayne, you are all such a help."

"Must be love." He laughs a hearty, resonant laugh.

"And you must be jealous," Fran says. Bayne is a gentle, small-boned black man, perhaps one-half Capricia's width.

"Oh, I am jealous," he says. "I'm ate to pieces by the green-eyed monster. But really, Fran?"

"What?"

"Don't hesitate to call the police if you need to."

"I'll just drive her to the mission myself," Fran says. "Or somewhere. It's already pouring rain over here."

She retrieves her keys from the living room. "It's a client from the shelter," she tells Carol, who remains wide-eyed but impassive. "I've got to take her somewhere to sleep. Or at least to Pico for a bus."

"There was thunder," Carol says. "It sounded like those guys on radio used to do it with sheets of aluminum. Joey's terrified of lightning, but he never would admit it." She gets up and follows Fran to the door.

"Hello, Capricia," Fran says as neutrally as possible.

"There you are!" Capricia grins. "I knew I'd make it. I told you I would, didn't I? How come you to live way over here in Mexikorea?" At thirty Capricia has been homeless on and off for years but prides herself on keeping to westside streets. She stands teetering on bright red, tiny-heeled slingbacks that match her damp and frilly acetate blouse, cut for cleavage down the belly. Fran can't help but think the word *bazooms*.

"How did you even get here?" she asks.

"I took the 33," Capricia says. "I took it to Western, but then I got me a ride."

"I bet you did," Fran says. "I thought you weren't doing that anymore."

"He was nice," Capricia says. "The body is not for fornication but for the Lord. He didn't want nothin' but a little gladhand. Then he drop me off over here at Taco Bell. Which is when the trouble started back with that dogshit."

"I'm going to give you a ride to the Sundown Mission," Fran says. "Or else to a bus stop so you can go where you want."

"Don't be cold now, Miss Fannie May. Lookie here what I got. You already said these bird-of-paradises was your favorites. I heard you say that, and here it is."

Fran hangs back, reluctant to accept the gift, dripping wet and obviously torn from a nearby yard.

"I've got the perfect vase." Carol steps from behind Fran to extend a long, pale arm for the flower, then disappears with it.

"See?" Capricia says. "You friend not near as cold as you try to be. If she you love-sister, she might not like me checkin' up like this."

"Don't mess with me," Fran says. "You're already in trouble enough. You'll be lucky if the mission has a bed this late."

"I heard that," Capricia says. "Why you think they call it Sundown? They lock you in that place at dark and kick you butt out in the crack of dawn. Don't nobody get in or out this late."

"Shit," Fran says.

"Shit is right, girl. Look at this knee." She lifts her leg delicately for Fran to see, miraculously maintaining her balance. There is an ugly gash with blood caked all around.

"I'll have to put some peroxide on that," Carol announces from the doorway. "Come in here." Fran shoots what's meant as a warning look, but Carol is already on her way to the bathroom with Capricia at her heels, trailing a yeasty whiff of wine.

"One of these big ol' red dogs," Capricia says. "What you call these big ol' red dogs? I could already see this ol' dog at the Taco Bell about to take a shit right where I was to be walkin' by. So I told this man to keep him away from the door till I got in, but he got right up in my face to laugh and somethin' told me to push him back, push him back. There was already dogshit under one of the cars, and this big ol' red dog made me twist my ankle, so I'm limpin' all the way over here. That's what they wanted to see, and that's what they got. It's not just here, either, but everywhere I go at."

Fran leans out the screenless window at the end of the corridor, catching rain in her palms and patting her face and neck, nearly inspiring a chill. The drag in her back means soon she'll bleed, a sporadic blessing that should bring relief. This intricate day seems to have wound itself past all reason into night. She stretches to touch the top of the window frame, then down to touch her toes. Every light is lit in the dilapidated cottage across the street, and the black-robed, elderly Mexican man who lives there is being helped into bed by a young female Sikh in luminous white. Fran will gather up imaginary energy, load Capricia into the Bug, and deliver her to Bayne for the night.

In the bathroom Carol and Capricia sit smoking long, brown Shermans, Capricia on the closed commode with an elaborate white gauze bandage around her knee, Carol on the edge of the bathtub, flipping ashes into the sink.

"Ashes to ashes and dust to dust," Capricia is saying. "But why you burn him up like that? You crazier than I am. How he spose to get up and dance in Heaven? He got to have some bones, at least. How come you to burn him up?"

"Capricia!" Fran says, but Carol is laughing.

"He told me to when he was in junior high school," she says. "He told me to burn him up and toss him into the waves. So that's what I'll do."

"We shall see the dead, small and great, stand up and dance before God," Capricia says. "I guess if the Lord can raise up the dead He can build back some bones if He has to. He delightest not in burnt offerings, though. The scriptures certify to that."

"Apparently he delighteth in killing off young boys before their time," Carol says. Her face has regained its hurting edge.

"Oh, it was that boy's time, all right," Capricia says. "You needn't to worry about that. You can rest assured it was that boy's time."

"How do you know it was his time?" Carol demands, in earnest but not with anger. "Just how do you know it was his stupid time?"

"He went, didn't he?" Capricia says. "That's the only time you go, when it's your time. You can't go no other way. If you go, it's your time, and if it's your time, you go. Ain't no use to quarrel over these truths we hold to be self-evident. Now he's baptized by fire among the children of the resurrection. An' he don't want his gorgeous mama sittin' here in the toilet bawlin' her eyes out, either."

"Well, that's true, he hates that," Carol says.

"Somethin' I always wanted to learn how to do was to learn how to surf," Capricia says, lifting the bad knee with one hand to guide it atop the good one. "I can just see me up there, shootin' them curls."

"Joey would teach you, too," Carol says. "He's that kind of kid. He wouldn't think a thing about taking you down to the water with him and getting you up on a board. You wanna do it? He says let's do it."

Fran has begun to feel like a chaperone, irrelevant at best, intrusive at worst. "Before you get ensconced here, Capricia, I have to call Bayne and tell him I'm bringing you back."

"I'm not goin' back to that Dennis the Menace," Capricia says. "He ack like I got dogshit on both shoes.

He too enthralled with his own self to care who be who or what be what." This is an accurate appraisal of Dennis, narcissism having driven him, perversely, to "help those less fortunate than himself." Fran tries not to laugh. "And that Bayne a little sparrowfart," Capricia adds. "He look like one good sneeze blow him away. These mens. You think it's the mens or the womens that break your heart the worst? Which one the worst ones to fall for?"

The question hangs suspended in the space between Fran and Carol, like a high lob in doubles that no one calls.

"I don't think it matters," Fran finally says. "Maybe we're all more trouble to each other than we're worth."

"It's just that you expect better of women," Carol says.

"I heard that," Capricia says. "The flesh lusteth against the spirit and the spirit up against the flesh. No fountain yields both salt water and fresh." As she reaches backward to flick her ash, she knocks a flattened saucer of soap off the back of the toilet. The shattering reverberates on inlaid tiles and jolts Capricia into begging forgiveness.

"I don't even care," Carol says. "Let's break something else." She picks up a thin pink drinking glass and tosses it into the tub for a high, crackling smash.

"Let's break this, then," Capricia says, reaching for a Mason jar full of drooping freesias.

"How about let's not," Fran says, stopping her hand. Suddenly the bathroom feels close as an elevator.

"You always so proper, Miss Fannie May. That's what I like. You always aimin' for the up-and-up."

"So let's go," Fran says. "Let's let Carol get some rest." She steps back and sees through the living room door that the bird-of-paradise stands in a lovely, tall vase on the floor in front of Joey's ashes.

"Capricia can stay here tonight if she likes," Carol says.

"That may not be such a good idea," Fran answers quickly. "You don't know Capricia, really. It might not be such a good idea."

"Do not forget to entertain strangers," Capricia says, "whereby some have entertained angels unawares. Hebrews, chapter 13, verse 2." Fran suspects this reference has been used to past advantage.

"I want her to stay if she wants to," Carol says.

"I cook the best spaghetti," Capricia declares. "And Carol has got to fatten up. All I need is a glass of wine and a jar of Ragu. This woman's belly has drawn up to her backbone. Eyes all sunk in. I got to call it a halt. Them that putteth their trust in the Lord shall be made fat."

"You wanna do it?" Carol says. "Let's do it."

Often when Fran awakes in a blast of heat she has the feeling she's burned through something that was in her way, but tonight the sound of rain confuses her. The wind has picked up, and she rises in darkness to spread newspapers beneath wide-open French windows throughout the apartment. She dips one hand into the living room bucket, not yet quite a whole inch full, then pulls on a pair of jeans. From the canvas chair in the breakfast nook she can watch rain angling through pale orange streetlight. As she leans forward her nipples come to rest on the tabletop, and she hears Brando warning Schneider that she'll get old like him and play soccer with her tits.

Before Fran woke up sweating she was at a party with her second husband, whose yelling drove her coatless down outer stairs and into a wintry parking lot. She could still hear him from there, though the words were indistinct, the whole situation more memory than dream. She had been dancing wrong with a guy, as she was inclined to do throughout that marriage. What strikes her now is the way Sam continued to yell long after she had quit the scene. She can't recall the dénouement. It took her three Wisconsin marriages to realize men bored her except for sex. At the sink she wets a washcloth and sponges neck and shoulders, belly and breasts. Flashes of lightning and occasional headlights illuminate Earth above the faucets. There is a crash next door, followed by whoops of laughter from Capricia, then Carol. Something is definitely cooking, garlic wafting thick on saturated air.

Fran winds her way back to the living room, turns on the end-table radio and stretches out on the couch, listening idly until Creedence gets into "Heard It Through

The Grapevine." A surge of energy rolls through her bare feet and along her legs until she is up and moving. *Honeyhoney, yeah.* Soon she is sweating from exertion as much as from a thermostat gone awry. *There must be some kinda way outta here.* Get up in the dark and dance while you got bones. *We are stardust, we are golden.* Suddenly, except for this music, whole decades seem to have gone up in flames behind her. *Gimme, gimme shelter.* Fran rushes to the bedroom for the stereo effect of a second radio, louder than is decent for the hour. She begins to pick an extremely mean guitar. *Rejoice, rejoice, we have no choice but to carry on.* She can feel a release of blood imploding deep in her swollen belly. Old moons and tides and women who bleed. *The lunatics are in my hall, I'll see you on the dark side of the moon.* Waves of sound keep swelling beneath her, curving out beyond the rain. *She's as sweet as Tupelo honey, she's an angel of the first degree.*

Jarring Light

Lately at home for Nola there has been the bitter, unmistakable odor of crushed lightning bugs. She has purchased a green plastic gadget called Enviroscan, purported to deodorize and generate negative ions, but now she's convinced that if she unzips her jacket, she'll find the scent has traveled with her from East Hollywood to the Glendale Galleria. Nola is hunched over a book and broccoli beef in the airless back room at Panda Express, and the food tastes odd, everything odd off cigarettes. It could be the broccoli that has her on edge with its crisp and pungent, stubborn green. She will concentrate on rice and tea.

For the moment she gives up reading and rereading a philosophical footnote that likens death to a burning library, an idea that seems to snag in her brain and block all metaphorical leaps. She thinks only of the drifter who set fire to the Central Library downtown, the stacks of wet or flaming books, the wounding image of a gutted structure. She wonders if the man might have held a grudge or was truly an arsonist at heart, pyromantic or pyromaniacal. Whatever he was, he is still on the loose.

At the St. Andrews branch, where Nola worked before quake damage shut it down, a man used to come
daily with his dog, an ordinary mongrel except for its
grossly swollen and discolored scrotum, which hung
nearly to the ground, likely weighing several pounds,
some kind of cancer no doubt to blame. The man would
park his red wagonful of newspapers inside the court-
yard door and tie the languid dog to the knob where
he could be monitored from Periodicals. One afternoon
Mrs. Laggert informed the man bluntly that his animal
was frightening children and would have to be removed.
Next morning, tall and gray and bristling with dignity
in his soiled white T-shirt, the man marched in and
pushed over most of the freestanding fiction shelves,
the domino principle serving him well. In charge at the
reference desk, Nola was so bedazzled by the noise and
spectacle that she neglected to buzz Security before the
fellow disappeared. Mrs. Laggert handled the police report, insisting the culprit would soon be caught in the
neighborhood. Weeks later Nola did glimpse him and
his empty wagon near the post office on Western Avenue, but she kept this wholly to herself. Probably the
dog had died by then.

She reopens her book, Sissela Bok's treatise on secrets,
to see if this sort of withholding of information might
be listed in the table of contents, but she can discern
no such category. The incident was based on a lie in
the first place, since the dog's balls were not frightening
children but embarrassing the prim and elderly Mrs.

Laggert. Nola has also read Bok's treatise on lying and considers scribbling a silly fan note on her soy-stained napkin: "Dear Doc Bok, I like *Secrets* even better than *Lying*. Obscurely, Nola Kinner."

For a glinting second she hears her mother's voice lilt toward her from a distant booth, though she squelches the impulse to look that way. She pours tea and imagines lighting a cigarette, then spears the last thin strip of beef instead and swabs her plate with it before she buries it under a dab of rice, neatly encircled by broccoli, and abandons it. Not reporting the dog-man has thrust her into complicity. She unzips her jacket halfway down and cautiously sniffs toward her breasts, reassured by a faint trace of sandalwood soap.

"Bonnie Louise, you have a yearning for perfection," a woman in the next booth says with remarkable sweetness to the seven- or eight-year-old beside her. "You have a yearning for perfection, kiddo."

Nola finds this touching but peculiar until she sees the fortune cookie. A yearning for perfection sounds so much better than merely being a perfectionist, a flaw in itself. Nola yearns for perfection. Or at least precision. "Persnickety from the get-go" is what her mother always said. She tries to picture sitting with her mother and hearing this fortune read aloud, her mother who, Nola is certain, never saw a fortune cookie, never tasted Chinese food in her thirty-nine years in Cairo, Illinois, and immediate points south.

Nola's own cookie alleges that at this very moment

someone is thinking good thoughts of her. Obviously, her rightful fortune got switched with the little girl's. She doubts anyone has thought good thoughts of her lately—since she quit smoking on her birthday last week she has mainly barked at people or kept to herself. Two years ago, in a fit of vigorous intention, she wrote a note and stapled it to her insurance policy, vowing that if she made it past her mother's age of death she would honor that fate by giving up tobacco, a bargain that strikes her now absurd, even if possible, with her muscles in rebellion, nerves chapped raw, brain dense as cotton. This morning, barely on simmer, her breakfast grits swirled up from the pan to scald the fleshy part of her thumb.

Sipping tea, Nola becomes aware she's being stared at. The child in the next booth sits with her chin cupped in her palms, gazing past her mother's dark, thick tangle of hair. Nola stares back until the girl finally blinks. "You're not as pretty as my mom," she says.

"That's true," Nola says. "I'm not as pretty as your mom."

"Bonnie, for Heaven's sake," the mother scolds, gripping her hand and rising to leave. "I don't know what gets into you."

"Her yearning for perfection must make her rude," Nola offers, not quite smiling, and the woman doesn't smile back, either, possibly offended at having been overheard. She shrugs toward Nola, then bends at the waist, as if this posture might absolve them both.

"I wonder if you could spare me one of those Winstons?" Nola says. "I seem to have come off without mine."

"No problem," the woman says, cheered by the request. She pops up two cigarettes and extracts one without touching the tip, a nicety that Nola appreciates, though as soon as she's alone she snaps off the filter, tamps the tobacco solid and sucks at the thing unlit before shredding it evenly over her plate.

On the escalator down to the car she gets dizzy and grips both rails. Near the exit she buys a pizza-size chocolate chip cookie and a carton of milk and finds a bench where she can eat. "Swimmy-headed," her mother would call it. She searches once again for Bok's footnote that will explain the main branch fire, how the death of a person is like the burning down of a great library as the inward connections of a life are lost, along with its holy, minute particulars. Driving home on Fountain Avenue, through Scientology's noxious blue ghetto of crosswalks, Nola begins to feel as if she is hearing again the terrible, thirty-year-old news.

At home her phone is ringing as she struggles with an obstinate deadbolt, scraping the knuckle she always scrapes if she tries to hurry turning the key. For nearly three years Richard has been her intermittently platonic downstairs neighbor.

"How's the smoking going?" he says. Nola has let him believe that his nagging concern influenced her decision to quit.

"You mean not smoking," she says, sucking gently at her wound.

"Yes, Miss Priss. I mean how is the not smoking going?"

"Strange," Nola says. "Everything is blurry, with weird odors all around the edges. Plus I keep burning myself and hearing my mother's voice. Otherwise, great."

"Saying what?" Richard asks. "What is your mother saying?"

"I don't hear words, only the voice. It's too complicated to explain."

"Well, *Goodfellas* is back at the Vista. Want to pop over and catch the eight o'clock?"

"Why does every third goddamn movie in America have to be about the goddamn mob?" Nola says, before the click and then dead air. She dials him back. "Sorry I raised my voice."

"I gather you don't want to see the film."

"I guess not. Sorry."

"I just read about these new patches you can get," Richard says. "These nicotine patches you paste on your arm or somewhere."

"Thrilling idea," Nola says.

"Or there's the gum. Nicotine chewing gum."

"Jesus. I'm not going to a doctor to purchase nicotine."

"Well, I'm just saying maybe you could use some help. I mean, you started chain-smoking corn silks when you were ten or something."

"Ha-ha, Richard. To you it's funny. You barely know what corn silks are."

"Well, when was the last time you tried to quit?"

"I've never tried to quit," Nola says. "I don't believe in trying to quit. I believe in either smoking or not smoking."

"I think I'll hang back up."

"Right," Nola says.

The lightning-bug odor is not quite present but not quite absent. She sniffs deep in the hallway closet before lighting jasmine incense. She can't recall ever seeing fireflies in southern California, but logically they're here, with the palm trees and magnolias and the mockingbirds. She slips off her sandals and situates herself among pillows on her bed. On TV Oprah Winfrey promises to be right back with an expert who will tell us all how to forgive the unforgivable, but Nola dozes off before she gets a chance to hear.

Aspirin won't touch the early morning headache, and, although she knows perfectly well there are no cigarettes in the house, Nola enacts a frantic, ritualized search in drawers and cupboards and closets, peering finally under the unmade bed where, after all, a stray butt might have rolled. Kneeling on the floor has a calming effect, and she is drawn to the space beneath the bed, lying flat on her back with only bare feet exposed to the room. This voluntary enclosure relieves some unnamed burden—she feels for the moment safe from herself. She pictures walking to the corner market and asking Armando for Pall Mall reds, but just as he puts them in her hand the craving passes. Suddenly the lightning-bug smell seems concentrated in the gauze that stretches across the bottom of the box springs, though she has such a bitter taste in her mouth, Nola wonders if it could be her breath or even residue inside her nostrils from decades of French-inhaling. There could be nicotine oozing out of her pores and, because it's an insecticide, the stuff might smell like bugs. She sees her father wetting a cigarette at the yellowed kitchen sink and shredding tobacco to rub on the bee sting over her eye. By then she was already sneaking Camels from his dresser and smoking with Buddy Alt at the creek. She reruns the trip to the store and asks Armando for Camels instead, the soft, squat pack diminished by his meaty, calloused palm. Her father would cup a burning cigarette until the ash fell off, then transfer this to the other palm in order to take a drag. At the end he'd go to the kitchen, brush his hands over the sink, run water on the butt, and toss it out the back door. He knew from the start that Nola was smoking but never once acknowledged it. In old age now, reduced to Garrett snuff and a Folgers coffee jar, he still ignores her as she smokes on the porch during rare visits back. Men who have brought their paychecks home from the mill get to say what's what, even if they don't always say it out loud: Only trashy women smoke and pierce their earlobes.

The fireflies were around all summer, and every so often she and Jeannie Swain would take a notion to catch some. Jeannie was the preacher's daughter, so Nola's mother would hunt them up a Mason jar apiece plus the icepick and hammer to gouge airholes. The things were pitifully easy to catch, their nature being to broadcast their exact whereabouts even before dusk. At first there would be no need to hurry or slam on the lid, though after a few, each new capture provided an opportunity for escape, so inevitably some got crushed in grooves with the turn of the cap. The white stuff that came out of their bellies looked like when you poked at the kernels of new sweet corn.

"Luciferin," Brother Swain told them once, aiming his eye significantly. "Luciferin is what they call that chemical that makes lightning bugs light up. And I know you girls know who old Lucifer is. So y'all better watch out now, hadn't you?" Nola can hear him laughing and can see the angle of his paunch as he turns to go up on the porch, can hear the wooden screen slam softly behind him, can make out the shadow of a chifforobe in the hall as he disappears behind it.

Her feet are freezing as she scoots from beneath the bed, pulls on socks, and brushes her teeth, concentrating on her tongue. Then she lifts Enviroscan from its bookshelf box, turns it on full force, and sets it as far back under the bed as she can reach.

At Ethical Drugs Nola stands boggled by a resplendent display of tobacco that stretches half the length of an aisle. She has stopped in for a pen refill but can't get past the cigarettes. Unwavering brand loyalty has kept her blind to this proliferation—lights and ultralights; browns and pastels; 100s and 120s; wide packs and flip-tops; wintergreens and charcoals; gimmicks, generics, and intricate filters. There are Mistys and Mores, Capris and Malibus, BelAirs and Montclairs, Bucks and Larks, Merits and Vantages, Eves and Nows. Nola suspects some of the brands may not contain tobacco and debates whether inhaling them could qualify as not smoking. Oddly, the Luckies still have L.S./M.F.T. on the pack ("Lucky Strike Means Fine Tobacco," though Jeannie Swain always chimed into the commercials with "Loose Straps Mean Floppy Tits, ha-ha"). Behind closed doors at home Brother Swain smoked sweet cherry cigars with white plastic tips that Jeannie and Nola played with but never actually lit. The summer her mother lay dying on the living room rollaway he had given Nola a special assignment for Sunday School, sending her to the bookmobile dictionary to research "the four big O's."

"If you learn the four O's, you'll pret-near know what you need to know about God," he said. Out of kindness or uneasiness he always aimed to keep Nola from getting bored at church. The next week she was well prepared.

"*Omnificent* means He created everything there is," she recited. "*Omniscient* means He knows everything there is to know. *Omnipotent* means He can do anything He wants to anytime He wants to do it. And *Omnipresent* means He's always everywhere at once."

"Real good, Nola. That's a real good lesson."

"And I found another one, too," she said. "*Omnivorous.* He can eat any plant or animal anytime He wants."

"Well, I reckon He can." Brother Swain tucked his chin and did not add the fifth O to his list on the board. "I reckon He can. It gives us all something to think about. Sounds to me like you're the one's got the omnivorous mind, though, sugar. You look that word back up and see if you don't."

"Sounds to me like He's the one making my mother sick," Nola said, and there the lesson ended.

She gravitates toward the snuff and chewing tobacco and sees that someone has torn the seal on a box of Sherman's Queen-Size Cigarettelos and lifted a few. She sniffs discreetly, nose level to the shelf, until she breaks into a gentle sweat. Her father would chew Beech-Nut and spit as he drove, a gob once boomeranging through the rear window and into Nola's ponytail. The coarse tobacco came in a thick, waxy pouch back then that made almost no crinkling sound.

At the end of the aisle Nola extracts a pack of Pall Mall reds from an open carton and scurries to the cashier, but the line is four deep and slow, everyone wanting stamps or lottery tickets. By the time it's her turn she has picked up a quarter-pound chocolate bar and relinquished the cigarettes to Dr. Scholl and the Odor-Eaters. In the car she tears into the candy and shamelessly devours it. *Have no other gods before me, for I am a jealous, omnivorous god who visits the sins of the fathers upon the daughters.* Nola remembers the refill but won't go back in.

At work Nola keeps catching glimpses of her mother's hem disappearing around corners. The dress is homemade, a deep blue plaid, with thin lines of black and gray and white. The cotton is rough, and Nola recognizes most positively the way it doesn't hang quite right, the way it lacks any natural flow. At first she watches for the woman, waits for her at the checkout desk to ask where she bought the material. But the woman herself never appears, only the trace of her skirt round this aisle or that and through various doors, behind the L-shaped card-file display. At one point it's certain she has entered the restroom beneath the stairway, but Nola finds only a couple of high school girls there passing a cigarette back and forth. She has sneaked many a drag down here herself and so refrains from the reprimand—the butt gets flushed in response to her silent gaze or, more to the point, her employee badge. When the girls leave, it's obvious the place is empty. Nola lingers inside the smell of smoke, with Pine-Sol and bug spray underneath.

"Either stay in or out," her mother whispers. "The house is filling up with mosquitoes."

Richard stands smirking at the array of merchandise spread across her bed. He takes up more space than Nola remembered, unnerving her with his solidity. "I've never seen you so carried away," he says. "I can't believe you actually bought all this stuff."

"I told you it was on sale," Nola says. "And with the staff discount it was a deal. Besides, all the money goes to help rebuild the main branch."

"I know, but look at this," Richard says. "Mugs and keychains and tote bags and flashlights? What are you going to do with five of these T-shirts?"

"One is for you," Nola says. "I mean if you want one."

"Oh. Sure. Thanks." He removes the shirt from its plastic wrap and holds it straight out for inspection. Against a maroon backdrop, the Central Library building logo is outlined in solid white. SAVE THE BOOKS looms large beneath. "It's great," Richard says, though both of them plainly see there's too much bright white rubber on the thing, stiffening the cotton and overplaying the message. Nola looks away as he peels off his plain black pullover, though she's curious about his chest hair, whether it's grayed any more since they last went to bed. Black is Richard's color, and maroon is not, but he stands in front of the mirror trying to look pleased. "Fits fine," he says, in spite of a puckering at the shoulders that means the shirt is not only too small but poorly stitched. Nola feels crushed by this and can't control her welling tears. "Really, hon, it's fine," he says.

"Don't be nice, Richard." She begins to gather items from the bed and repack them into a cardboard box. "I guess I can always sleep in the damn things."

"Since when do you sleep in anything? You're not

really crying over this, are you? Let me pay you for a couple of mugs."

"Stop being nice. You're making my head explode. Just take off the shirt and leave it in the box."

Richard obeys and follows her into the living room.

"Put your other shirt back on," Nola says. "I'm crazy enough."

Richard lets out an explosive sigh but cooperates, then keeps his distance across the room. "How many days now?" he says. "I know it's over a week."

"Eleven days," Nola says.

"Fantastic! Eleven days is wonderful. I'm proud of you. Congratulations."

"Don't cheer me on. I'm afraid I'm going to kill someone. I practically screamed at Margie this morning over a misshelved magazine. Does it smell funny in here to you?" She plops onto the couch, massaging her temples with her palms. Enviroscan seems to be on the blink.

"I don't smell anything," Richard says. "Actually the air's a lot better up here now. What's going on?"

"I'm in a time warp," Nola says. "Like there was this billfold when I was little? This tooled leather billfold at the dime store that had spurs and a cowboy cactus etched on it. One of those pale calf things that zip all around. Which my mother wouldn't buy for me, I don't know why, she just flat out refused. So I took my Mother's Day money and bought it for her. I felt so ashamed when she opened it up."

"What did she say?"

"She said she liked it. She acted like she liked it. All week I've been obsessing about what happened to it. She must have eventually let me have it, but I can't remember using it or where it ended up. All I can really remember is how I felt when she opened it and we both saw how selfish I was."

"My God, Nola, you were a child. Maybe you liked it so much, you did think she'd like it. Besides, it's what we all do half the time anyway, isn't it, give gifts we really want for ourselves? It's practically the golden rule of gift-giving."

Nola watches him lean into the kitchen doorway and soothingly stroke his dark, wiry beard. She feels a surge of affection—for the softhearted Jew, so unself-consciously attuned to limitations in the best of intents. "Tell me something funny, Richard," she says. "Tell me one of your excellent, instructive jokes."

"All you need is a good laugh, baby." He attempts a leer but can't quite pull it off, which does amuse her. "I saw this bumper sticker today," he says. "GEORGE, THE ONLY BUSH WITH BALLS."

"The only Bush with balls?" Nola says. "What is that supposed to mean, that his son's don't have any? Or just that he got us into a war?" Richard is laughing at her, or at least at her exasperation. "It doesn't even make sense. Shouldn't it say *a* Bush with balls? What does *the only* Bush even mean? Was it one of your ESL students? Was it in the college parking lot? Maybe it's a translation problem."

"*Bush* is a female word," Richard says. "Don't you remember the campaign buttons that said LICK BUSH?"

"Cute," Nola says. "Why is it a female word? I thought it was pubic hair. Anybody's pubic hair."

"A man has a bush, sure, but a woman *is* a bush," Richard says. "By definition, I mean."

"By definition?" Nola says. "You're a bigger pig than I ever imagined. Exactly what do you think you're saying?"

"Calm down," Richard says. "I don't mean my own definition. I can't help the way the word is used. I mean, it's on the order of *hair-pie* or *hairburger*. You know, *the bearded clam.*"

"God. Where are you getting this crap?" When he won't stop laughing, Nola slings a pillow that bounces off his shoulder and clatters silverware across the kitchen table behind him. "Are you saying he was pussy before the Gulf War but now he's got balls? Is this what's supposed to get him reelected?"

"I'm not saying anything," Richard says. "You're killing the messenger. You're cutting off the messenger's bushwhacker." He doubles over laughing, hands on his knees.

"You're trying to make me smoke," Nola says, verging on tears. "You are. You're trying to see if I'll smoke. Jesus."

"No, I'm not," Richard says, quickly serious. "I don't want you to smoke. It's such a relief not to hear you cough. You know I don't want you to smoke. How can you even say such a thing? I know you're having a hard time. I just hate to see you lose your sense of humor."

"I haven't lost my damn sense of humor. All I'm saying

is that GEORGE, THE ONLY BUSH WITH BALLS is the product of a muddled mind. Will you give me that, at least? That it's stupid?"

"Of course it's stupid," Richard says. "It's not meant to be taken seriously."

"When you purse your lips that way," Nola says, "your mouth becomes a bearded clam."

"Hairsplitter," Richard says, not smiling. "That's another word for prick. Look it up if you don't believe me."

"So now you're calling me a prick," Nola says.

"You said it, not me. But you do have a knack for splitting hairs."

"Go home, Richard. Before I choke you."

On his way out through the bedroom Richard retrieves the library T-shirt. "Maybe your father remembers," he says. "Maybe your father remembers what happened to the cowboy wallet."

"Believe me, it's not a thing he would know," Nola says. "Besides, he's too deaf now for the phone. Unless it's our prescribed exchange."

"Which is what?" Richard says.

"The weather," Nola says. "Or what his wife is cooking or refusing to cook. And whether I still like to read. He always asks me if I still like to read, as if I might suddenly not anymore. It's his way of apologizing for trying to stop me as a kid. He always hated to see me reading. Or maybe he can't think of anything else to say to me."

"Well, you're not altogether an easy woman to talk

to, Nola," Richard says. "He worked his butt off in a
factory all his life. Why don't you give the guy a break?"

"Fuck you, Richard."

"Whatever you say, sweetheart. Just call me Dick, why
don't you?"

"Good-bye, Dick," Nola says. "And don't you ever come
back up here unless you bring me a carton of cigarettes."

Nola wakes up clawing at her knees, skin ablaze with
itching. She jerks back the covers and snaps on a light but
can see no sign of whatever is biting, in fact can see no
bites at all but only the redness left by her nails. Neverthe-
less she gets up and brushes both hands firmly across all
the bedding. She can't grasp the dream, if there was a
dream, but senses she may have been hiding in her mother's kitchen pantry, lined with translucent quarts of peach
and pear preserves. Nola cradles herself in pillows and
reaches for night-table cigarettes, their absence jolting her
wider awake. So this is what habit means, humiliation.
What about the habits of nuns, and what about humility?
She tries to focus on these connections while her body
quietly pitches a nicotine fit, exuding a clammy sweat that
brings on chills. She pulls the covers up to her neck, then
over her head till she can't stand the stink.

At a gas station register on her way home she purchased a single Marlboro for twenty cents, what used
to be the price of a pack. Back at the car without a
light she tried to get one from passersby, who refused

to break pace or look at her, certain she must be begging for cash. Red-faced, she gave the cigarette to a street man watching her from his bus-bench camp. Nun's habits, riding habits. Riding crops, tobacco crops. Habitats and habitations. Lamplight accentuates her smoke-yellowed walls. Richard once offered to paint the whole apartment if she would quit, though naturally she declined. She tries deep breathing, which seems to help, but somehow the air is acrid going out, if not coming in. Fireflies light up for the mating dance.

Most summers, when they heard the picking was good, she and her parents would drive across the river into Kentucky, through soybean and burley tobacco fields, into knotty woods for blackberries. They would set out soon after sunup, fill every bucket and pot in the house, and be home well before noon, soaking the berries and scrubbing purple fingers. The afternoon would swell with tart, sweet heat from the stove, and by suppertime the flimsy back-porch table would sag with pints of cooling jam. Most summers, this was, until Nola got chiggers and, as her father said, "put the quietus on blackberrying." He acted as if it were her own fault, which seemed fair enough, since no one else fell prey. Kids at school would get impetigo, but chiggers burrowed in and seemed much worse. By the second night Nola scratched herself bloody and had to be painted and poulticed up.

"You went and got yourself eat up good," her father said, bringing to boil a large pan of water, dumping in half a can of rough-cut Granger (in winter he smoked a meerschaum, even with the house closed up). When the brew had steeped, Nola stood naked on a kitchen chair while he slathered it on with a small paintbrush, everywhere the welts were, which was everywhere elastic had been. Her mother drew deep breaths and blew at her constantly, hoping to distract her and cool the fire.

"No use to cry now," her father said. "What's cured will cure you and damp down that sting. If it kills the mites, it'll kill the pain."

Nola's mother cut up cheesecloth, then soaked and wrung it out to pin round her waist and groin, and ankles, too, where her socks left off. Nola had to wear winter pajamas, tops and bottoms, so she couldn't scratch through in her sleep. Next morning she was rank and crusty and sore but better, and her daddy told her he had told her so.

It is barely 4:00 A.M. but Nola decides to shower and start the day. She chooses milk-and-honey soap from her assorted basketful, letting water run over her for several slow minutes. Later with coffee and a book she sits staring into daybreak out her living room window. Two skinny young Latino boys appear on bikes and begin to spray the building across the street. They are wearing baggy Bermudas and the kind of sleeveless undershirts her father always wore. They trade off the paint can, taking turns holding up the bicycles, and they leave the wall covered with tall, black, spidery letters: ACE and LOONEY, GHOST and BONES. Were they up this early or out all night? Nola sighs and keeps on trying to read—she's been bogged down in *Secrets* and has switched to Erving Goffman's *Asylums*. The libraries now are full of lost children. In gourmet shops, real blackberry jelly sells for five or six dollars a jar. Whoever does the picking no doubt gets well underpaid. She makes a note to look up *nolo contendere*.

Nola has fixed herself a sandwich at the kitchen table. These days she is drinking less coffee and eating less often standing up, making an effort to savor food itself, unprovoked by attendant urges to smoke. This morning she managed to conquer inertia and clear the drainer of scoured ashtrays, stacking them onto a high, back shelf. Out the window she's been following the slow progress of an elderly señora with groceries balanced on her head, up the long hill north on Normandie. Nola imagines the steeper the hill, the farther forward the woman will need to lean, but at this distant angle it's impossible to tell. Perhaps the secret is to keep yourself straight.

Reaching for her sandwich she undergoes the peripheral but distinct impression that someone is with her at the table. She is not exactly frightened but reluctant to exhale, as if the slightest current might disperse the radiant guest. Without hesitation her mother lifts the sandwich from Nola's hand, takes a dainty bite, and sets it back onto the saucer. She is wearing her black-and-white, Sunday, store-brought dress, a simple cotton crêpe, dramatically square at the neck.

"Hmmm," she says. "What is that?"

"Avocado," Nola says.

"Avocado," her mother says. "Pretty rich. Pretty color. What's that bread?"

"It's a seven-grain bread," Nola says.

"Seven grains in one bread," her mother says. "Chews about like wood pulp."

"There's Miracle Whip on it, though," Nola offers. "Miracle Whip Light, actually."

"Miracle Whip isn't what it used to be."

"No, it isn't," Nola agrees. "But I keep on buying it."

Her mother retrieves the sandwich, settles her elbows on the table and takes another bite, chewing slowly, ruminating. Nola is simultaneously aware that her mother is eating the sandwich and that it lies untouched on the plate, a fact that she finds neither comforting nor disturbing. What disorients her is that she and her mother are the same age and size, sitting with identical posture, speaking identical tones, raising and lowering heavy-lidded gray eyes. Her mother used to let Nola roll up that coarse brown hair, twisting strands around two tiny fingers, then flattening curls against the scalp, crisscrossing each one with bobby pins. For years Nola did her own hair that way. "We favor," she says quietly, reaching back for the word.

"We favor a right smart," her mother says, continuing

to eat. After a while she announces, "They have these tests now, these mammeograms."

"Mammograms," Nola says.

"You know how to say it, but you don't know how to go get yourself one." Her mother lays the sandwich down and reaches for the inside hem of her dress in front, dabbing delicately at her mouth with it.

"I know how to get one," Nola says, no longer quite adult in pitch. "I can get one anytime I want."

"Maybe so, but you haven't yet. And you don't look like you're about to, either."

"You should talk," Nola says. "You wouldn't go till your tit was half eaten up because Daddy said it would get better on its own." Nola shocks herself with this, something she hardly knew she knew. "I should have made you go myself," she adds.

"He couldn't stand the thought of them cutting on me, honey," her mother says. "He's never been to a doctor in his life. It's not any call for you to talk so ugly."

"You're the one who listened to him," Nola says, now thoroughly the snotty and petulant child.

"Well. Maybe I didn't want them cutting on me, either. And maybe I did hope and pray it would go away. Or maybe I knew it was already too late." She gives Nola a steady, painstaking lookover. "We were ignorant as all get-out," she says finally. "What's your excuse? Being mad at us over it? What good's a big IQ if you're just all pouty and contrary? Come here and hug my neck. Let me give you some sugar."

Nola feels herself rise and climb into the roomy softness of her mother's lap to cry. She can sense soft kisses on the top of her head. She returns to her own chair grown back up.

"Have you got any Eagle Brand condensed milk?" her mother says. "We could make you a lemon icebox pie."

"I can run get some if you'll wait," Nola says.

"I can't wait, honey. You'll have to make it yourself. You'll remember once you start. Anyhow, the recipe is on the can. You'll have to get you a graham cracker crust and that RealLemon, you know, that used to come in those shiny plastic lemons? You and Jeannie Swain always tried to use them for water guns. Reconstituted lemon juice. I never did know exactly what that was."

"I don't know what it is, either," Nola says.

"Something somebody whomped up to sell," her mother says. "But don't try fresh lemons or the pie's not near as good. And don't you be smoking those old coffin nails anymore, either, Nola. They're filthy and nasty and make you sick all over."

"I'm not, Mamma," Nola says.

"They wrinkle your face up, too. Here you are such a pretty girl and already got fag lines on that upper lip. It's not even ladylike. I don't want you sucking on those things."

"I won't, Mamma."

"Don't tell me you won't if you will, now."

"I won't, Mamma. I think I may have already quit."

"And I swear, Nola, this Richard boy. You act like you're blind in one eye and can't see out the other." Nola laughs a silent but hearty laugh and then, beginning to fade, her mother says, "Finish your sandwich," which Nola does without protest.

April evolves into early June, and Nola mails an eightieth-birthday package to her dad: Enviroscan, with a new box of filters; two Central Library coffee mugs; and all the makings for lemon pie (along with thanks in advance to Estelle). She's engrossed in von Franz on redemptive fairy tales and bikes to work alternate days if there's no smog alert. She has taped two recent cookie fortunes onto her refrigerator door: A FROWN WILL KEEP THE OTHER AWAY and JUDGEMENT A LITTLE OFF AT THIS THYME.

In a distant corner at Ultracare, Nola and Richard have claimed the last two cushioned chairs in the long and crowded waiting room. Newcomers now will have to sit on hard, molded plastic near the central elevators. Oddly, the soft seats face away from the reception cubicle, so in order to see the technicians who burst through swinging doors to call patients, Nola has to keep vigil over her shoulder. "I'll sit here and miss my name," she tells Richard, "and end up blowing the damn appointment."

"Don't worry," he says. "One of us is bound to hear it."

Above and to their right a blue-and-white TV screen

intones computer-voiced facts about preventive health care—the necessity for rectal probes and Pap smears, supportive shoes and sunscreens, proper diet and eye exams. "My God," Nola says. "Are you listening to this? Even if you do get the test, there's one glaucoma that can strike you abruptly blind. We live in a cruel universe, Richard. Have you ever noticed that?"

"It's very humbling, isn't it?" Richard says. "I guess it's how we got religion."

Nola searches his face for irony and, finding none, acknowledges the fact that what she always thought eroded faith might also serve to provoke it. "Lucifer matches," she says. "That's what my father called those kitchen matches that would strike anywhere. He used to strike them on his pant leg. I could never really fathom the tale about the Angel of Light and the Prince of Darkness."

"I guess it makes sense they're both the same guy," Richard says. "Why don't you relax for a minute? Sit back and take a breath. You're getting this routine mammogram. You have no reason to think there's anything wrong. The pictures will just confirm what you already know."

"What you don't know is the point," Nola begins, but lets it drop.

"Here, look at this," Richard says. "Can you believe this?" He passes her a magazine that features two lists of celebrity women: those who've had breast "enhancements" and those who have had "reductions."

Disgusted, Nola is compelled to study each name. "All I want is for mine to stay exactly as they are," she says.

"Me, too." Richard won't look away until he gets a smile. "Remember Steve Martin saying he could never be a woman because he'd just stay home all day and play with his breasts?"

"The ultimate mammacentric American male," Nola laughs.

"You're looking beautiful," Richard says. "All bright-eyed and clear and soft, like your skin is luminescent."

"I'm so jumpy," Nola says. "I never knew I was so nervous. Such a fraidy-cat, really. I feel like I need more practice at everything. It's embarrassing to be this old. Plus the craving can still set me off."

"What's the perfume?" Richard says. "It must be new. I like it."

"You do?" Nola beams, wearing no fragrance beyond oatmeal soap. "What is it you like?"

"You smell sunny. You smell the way your skin looks. Lean over here a second."

Nola keeps her distance, glancing around the room. She waits while a technician calls three women at once. "I might be next," she says. "It seems like we've been here hours. I haven't thanked you for coming with me."

"You're very welcome," Richard says coolly. *"De nada."*

"I just think it might be a mistake to stir things up again," she whispers.

"You always put it that way," Richard says. "The truth is it's a mistake ever to let things go unstirred."

They sit in silence for a while, pretending absorption in magazines.

"This is going to sound silly," Nola whispers. "Don't laugh. Well, you can laugh if you want. But I've never been to bed with anyone as a nonsmoker. There's something scary about it."

"I was thinking about that last night," Richard says. "But it might be wonderful. Like losing your virginity, only a whole lot better. Trust me."

"Trust you," Nola says. "There's a line."

"Besides," Richard says, "I got you these." He unzips his jacket and produces an authentic pack of paper-covered chocolate cigarettes. "Old Golds," he says. "Remember those ads with the Old Golds tap dancing, those girls with long, gorgeous legs? That's all you could see, like they must have been completely naked underneath those huge cigarette boxes. That really turned me on as a kid. They seemed so amazing on our grainy black-and-white. Now it sounds bizarre."

Nola is examining the gift, the sparkle of the cellophane. "I think I may have to give you some sugar," she says.

"Give me some candy?"

"Give you some sugar. It's an old expression." She leans to kiss his cheek and then his neck below the beard. They both jump up when her name is called.

No Man's Land

Corinne has lugged a second bucket of water downstairs to pour across hot concrete. Suffused with chlorine, it doesn't really smell like rain, of course, but still it pleases, suggesting at least the watering of a lawn, as if grass were possible in front of this building. She squints at the sidewalk, watching the dark, shallow puddle elongate and disappear with undue speed. Parched winds from the desert have flattened her hair dramatically.

She cups her hands above her eyes to search the street for a mail truck. Her unemployment check should have come yesterday, but instead there was the crisp, white, oblong box addressed in thick, black, calligraphic print, unmistakably Jack's. Something possessed him, almost seventeen years beyond their divorce, to send Corinne her girlhood tennis racket. Scarred blond wood with a jagged tear across its sweet spot, the thing emits persistent vibrations and kept her awake much of the night. Now three deliberate cups of Cuban coffee have set her abuzz with unfocused anticipation, though the runic stone she drew this morning, like yesterday's, indi-

cated STANDSTILL. The check may or may not arrive.
She may or may not walk it to the bank. Corinne situates herself on the bottom step and extracts sunglasses
from the pocket of her skirt. Gold round bifocals, the
darkest of tints, they have a cooling and calming effect.
Five days in a row near a hundred degrees and minimal
respite overnight.

Halfway up Serrano an ice-cream truck glides along
the curb, blaring "It's Only a Paper Moon" in "La Cucar-
acha" tempo. The driver has slowed behind a frail Korean woman who, with obvious effort, is pushing an
uncased cello uphill in a shopping cart. She tries to
wave him by, but he seems reluctant to pass until she
halts, turns the cart into a driveway, and covers her ears
with both hands, prompting him both to accelerate and
lower his volume. Corinne leans forward to peer at a
familiar, battered green pickup that is rounding the corner, stacked higher than its cab not with the usual tire-
flattening load of filthy mattresses, but with yard-long
loofahs, lighter than the breeze. At the stop sign the
stout, mustachioed driver steps out to check his cords
and hooks. From the opposite direction the stink of
warm garbage precedes a rusty gray mechanical rig
marked quaintly CIVIC RUBBISH. Jack would bake bread
on Saturdays, sometimes coarse, flat loaves so richly
laden with garlic that the flavor would not only linger
on the breath but exude from the pores through a day
or two of sweat.

The winter of the spiritual life is upon you, the rune book said. *There's a freeze on useful activity. Shed, release, cleanse away the old. Be still, surrender, and watch for signs of spring.*

Corinne recognizes one of her short-term remedial students from several semesters ago rolling a Dumpster toward the garbage truck and fitting it onto the forklift. The young man has retained the stooped shoulders and rounded hips of his early adolescence so that, although he is well over six feet tall, he appears unsuited to such physical work. As the truck advances, he hangs on by one arm and waves at her with the other.

"Good morning, Ms. Wade."

Corinne is pleased by this, since the circumstance does not require him to notice or remember her, much less speak. She broadly waves and smiles, annoyed to find she can't think of the boy's name, which sits just behind her eyelids in boldface caps she can't discern. "You have a mighty hot job today," she shouts against the noise of the compactor, but this rings hollow without his name. As he disappears behind her building, she recites the alphabet to herself, hoping for a light-bulb effect when she hits the right first letter. *LMNOP.* Could be *Martin* or *Maurice.* Call him the gangster of love, call him Maurice. Not it.

"At least I even got a job," the boy says when he reappears. His damp black T-shirt sports a hot pink gothic *X* across his heart.

Corinne does not disclose her own unemployment, since even though L.A. Unified is collapsing on itself, she is hoping to be reassigned by midsummer. She does not allow herself to comment, either, on how this child has grown a foot since she saw him last. And she mustn't reveal she's forgotten his name. All this inhibition results in an awkward lull.

"I could still tell you things you've only read about on TV." The boy grins as he swings himself back onto the truck.

Corinne laughs and dismisses him with both hands in mock disgust. He once cracked her up with this remark during a class discussion about the value of books in relation to life experience—her usual pitch and plea for the importance of learning to read. At least he remembers something from the class, his own accidental joke if not his teacher's earnest words of wisdom. *Lewis,* maybe.

"That's the trouble, Lewis," she had said. "You only want to read about it if it's on TV." Another day he had asked her suddenly, "What is your stereotype, Ms. Wade?"

"You mean the stereotype of a female WASP?" she said.

"No, I mean what type of stereo do you have?" He took her laughter for the approval he craved, and she had let it go at that, though now she thinks perhaps she shouldn't have. *Lewis* doesn't sound quite right. The unrelenting white-hot sun is clarifying her irrelevance. *Leon* or *Leonard. Lamont* or *Lawrence.* "Read that sentence aloud for us, Lawrence." The kid will not comply because his name doesn't even begin with *L.* For a moment Corinne leans in the kitchen doorway, watching Jack knead dough, flour settling in the blond hair above his wrists. He will laugh and repeat himself, how if he didn't have tenure, he'd never dare step on campus reeking so mightily of garlic. Sweaty and beginning to freckle, Corinne retrieves her bone-dry bucket and climbs two flights of narrow stairs.

On and off for years now, whenever she sticks her head under a faucet to wash her hair, Corinne is treated to the image of Jack's plastic-covered shirts on hangers, fresh from the cleaners, draped over the backseat of their old Beetle. Blue and white oxford button-downs, nothing more than that. Soak the hair and see those shirts, time and time again, a singularly unevocative display. In biology, memory is supposed to be what modifies behavior after experience, though in plastics it's what makes a thing return to its prior shape after being deformed. (Get a bit of moisture back into the desert air and each hair on her head will remember how to curl.) On PBS an Alzheimer's patient achieves complete amnesia every ninety seconds, making a mockery of "live in the now." Memory would seem to be who we are and who everyone is to us, but Corinne watched a naked brain laid out and sliced upon a metal table, revealing cross sections of hippocampus in perfect seahorse profile, the memory bank itself shaped like a mythical creature ridden by gods. This is what she reads about on TV. They say the brain doesn't know the difference

between an actual experience and an imagined or remembered one, at least in terms of chemicals.

If *Montgomery* were a two-syllable name, *Montgomery*
would be it. These lapses come with middle age, the
forgetting as random as the remembering. Did she or
did she not water the plants last night? Not long ago
she'd have known the answer without having to check
and check again and finally write it down. Her refrigerator is stocked with perfume-flavored, raspberry ginger
ale, whose can design she mistook for 7-Up. One man
mistook his wife for a hat. A research clinic in Long
Beach will pay nine hundred dollars if you have the
right nepenthic symptoms.

What made Jack hold on to the racket all these years,
through another marriage and several moves? Corinne
is sure she could call him up and get an uncomplicated
answer ("It belonged to you. I didn't think I should
throw it away.") And why send it to her now? ("It was
yours. I thought you might like to have it.") Jack played
straightforward tennis, point by point by point, studying
Ken Rosewall on how to spare his aging legs.

You may find yourself entangled in a situation to whose implica-
tions you are blind. A chill wind is reaching you over the ice
floes of old habits. The symbol on the STANDSTILL rune
looks suspiciously like a capital *I*.

Corinne unplugs her phone, disinclined to discuss anything whatsoever with anyone at all, though an hour ago
she was exasperated to reach Ginger's machine instead of
Ginger. The telephone is a mystery but less so than a re-

corder. You say some words that stick to tape and abide there patiently, indefinitely, in hope of a future hearing. She had called with some urgency to correct a mistake from dinner Sunday night, when a long and winding conversation had touched upon artistic technique.

"They always use Mantegna's dead Christ to illustrate perspective," Corinne had said, with no response around the table. No one seemed to recognize the allusion, but this morning she remembered *foreshortening*, it was *foreshortening* she had meant to say, and perhaps all the young guests were being polite, since only Ginger knew her well. But how do you explain *foreshortening* to an answering machine? She hadn't waited for a beep.

"You've got a mighty hot job today, *blank*." For a second, *Lincoln* is it, except she has already ruled out *L*. Out the window the Korean woman is being pulled back downhill by the cello-in-a-cart. The ice-cream truck has switched to "Bicycle Built for Two," and the scene evokes Technicolor Fellini, with Sisyphean comic verve. Corinne soaks a paper towel at the sink and spreads it, dripping, across her face and head. She will lie down again, despite the caffeine.

Upright against a bare white corner the tennis racket inhabits her bedroom as solidly as a piece of antique furniture. Corinne rouses herself to set it in the hallway closet but instead extracts a trophy (GRANITE WOMEN'S SINGLES CHAMP/1970) from behind a stack of stale boxes and spends twenty minutes searching for the miniature gold-plated racket that slips in and out of the tiny fist of a slender, skirted figure, poised atop her pedestal to execute a smash. Corinne sets this relic on a shelf above her desk and senses a further depletion of air in the room, despite the fan. Yes, she had been that slim, almost, and she and Jack took mixed doubles that year, too, the summer before Lela came to town, their marriage still in the pre-Lela phase. At least he didn't mail her the two-figured trophy as well. She likes imagining he's got it tucked away somewhere in his univeristy office, that he peeks at it every few years, that he never mentions it to his wife. Or of course he may have tossed it. In truth, these awards were testimony less to their prowess at the game than to the fact that all the top-notch players in Granite had joined the new Racquet Club outside of town that year, snubbing the tournament on city courts. "We're the best damn players in town," Jack laughed. "Among the professorial paupers."

Divorced seventeen years, married twelve, age difference fifteen. This means Jack is sixty-three years old and that she's now his age the year she left him, a dreadful age to be abandoned, though he soon secured himself a new wife. Jack is married to this Wife Number Three, and Corinne, because all this time for her it's been only women, Corinne is probably still married to Jack. She stares at the trophy and lets this visceral truth resettle over her like dust. There are dishes in her kitchen that they ate together from. She runs a tall glass of water at the bathroom sink and drinks it down, then fiddles with the fan to maximize its oscillation across her bed. Why does *Montgomery* keep sounding right when she knows *Montgomery* isn't it?

The racket is nearly forty years old, the upper rim worn flat from scooping balls off the court instead of bending to pick them up, or rushing in to meet low volleys instead of waiting for the top of the bounce. Corinne can feel how her body used to execute these moves with ease, tomboy that she was, unafraid to hurl herself or lunge to greet a passing shot. She must have been nine the summer she strode into Mullins Hardware and emptied her cowboy blue bandana of more than ten dollars in change, announcing, "I want the Little Mo one." The outline of a face is still discernible at the base of the rim and, though her features have faded, you can still read most of the letters in the official "Maureen Connolly" signature.

Corinne played with girlfriends on asphalt courts in the park every summer until eighth grade, when Bobby Bodeen began insisting she go on "tennis dates," an eccentric idea to her at the time. Bobby Bodeen, with his good manners and bad skin, took the game much more seriously than his talent for it justified, discombobulating Corinne, who didn't want to embarrass him by winning, or herself by losing. When she got control she played it smart, setting up lobs for Bobby to smash, deliberately never acing a serve. Once on the way out for a Coke,

Corinne looked into a parked car and saw the man who had been on the court next to theirs sitting behind the wheel with his shorts off, penis in hand. Maybe the man was just overheated and not perverse, but suddenly tennis felt too complicated and perplexing. She spent high school summers lolling about the pool in the park, flirting and letting boys "teach" her how to swim, which to this day she's never properly learned.

She played no more tennis until Jack dragged her out on the courts her senior year in college, after she'd been through his Philosophy class, after he'd moved out of a lukewarm marriage and into motel heat off campus with her. At thirty-five, Jack was a steady, graceful player whose strength and rationality gave him an edge over youth and her tendency to repeat mistakes. She could play her best against him and still win only often enough to keep it interesting for them both. Corinne stuck with the old wooden racket for years after they were married, right up until the summer they met Lela, in fact, when she gave in to fashion and bought a steel one, expecting miraculous improvements in her game that never did materialize. Nowadays it's hollow, high-tech graphite and space-age plastic, heads so large they look as if the sweet spot must be doubled. Call Maurice the Space Cowboy. Call Lela the racketeer of love.

Photographic memory is supposed to be when memory is precise and lasting as a snapshot, though photos serve as memories themselves. Some years ago in a thrift shop Corinne came across a framed eight-by-ten black and white of someone's backyard court, nothing but the court itself, serene from above and slightly to the left, the surface pitch with stark, fresh lines. She stood staring at it so long, a clerk approached to ask if she was ill, and in fact it had made her ill and slightly dizzy, the way it threw her life into violent relief, deceptive in its vision of orderly containment, uncomplicated rules, prescribed behavior, all the accoutrements of certainty. An empty court excludes the players and what it means to win or lose. The court knows nothing of confidence, nothing of self-doubt, nothing of domination or cheating or the insidious power of self-loathing. An empty court is here and now and timeless, unsullied by the human need to replay the last point or anticipate the next while the one in motion whips you by. Devoid of play, the court is monastic, superior to the fleshy bodies that must execute the game, superior to the struggle and everything at risk.

When Corinne first moved from Granite to Los Angeles, she would use her steel racket to beat at Lela's imaginary face, not the actual face but a photograph, and not the photo itself but her memory of it, a photo she still keeps somewhere (small carved box, top dresser drawer). It's a shot Jack took one Sunday afternoon, an unapologetic, sexy pose, barefoot in front of their fireplace, hands in skirt pockets, no trace of smile. Corinne would chop till she saw the image in bits on the mattress, no bloodshed or permanent disfigurement required for one so elusive as Lela. Even now Corinne imagines her at tennis much more easily than in bed.

The amazing thing about Lela on court was the way she always appeared to be moving more slowly than she actually was, disconcerting at first for both partners and rivals. This optical illusion enabled her to become a master of the misdirected shot—she would get herself to the ball in time to return it in the least expected direction, leaving opponents dead in their tracks or running like crazy in impotent surprise. This strategy came naturally to Lela, though she certainly refined it more and more to her gain. Lela was nearly five-nine and had those lovely long legs some taller women have that are perfectly flat-straight down the back, not curving in much at the knee. Tennis skirts cast her as all leg in motion, deceptive and distracting as you tried to gauge her speed. To play in the heat she would put her hair up, braiding it into one long coil to twist around the top of her head. The effect was darkly innocent milkmaid or sophisticated Bergman actress, the very presence of such a braid an invitation to unpin it, loosen the hair and let it fall. It was Lela's habit to keep unbuttoned one button below modesty on anything she wore, so even a baggy Hawaiian shirt enticed enough to provoke a second look.

"You know who's really, really attractive?" a party lech from History once asked Corinne, having cornered her for hours with no exit line in sight.

"Besides me, Phil?" she asked, tired of passing him hors d'oeuvres.

"In addition to you, sweetheart." He was slurring his words.

"Lela Porter," Corinne said, abandoning him to his scotch.

"But how did you know?" he called after her.

"Eyesight," she threw back. "How do you think?"

Lela was wearing a low-cut black sheath that evening, thick, dark auburn hair hanging down past where her bra would have fastened, if she's been wearing one. Corinne could never figure out her wardrobe, which seemed a mix of thrift-shop hippie and best-store elegant. And Corinne never knew anyone else who wore a tennis glove.

Most admirable was Lela's ability to concentrate on the ball, actually to watch the ball instead of the person who hit it, a persistent weakness in Corinne's own game. It was on a tennis court that they first met, each having been invited separately for doubles by two other faculty wives. That summer the game had come into its full-fad, early-seventies swing, and the university courts were jammed from early morning till ten at night, when the lights went off automatically. Corinne resented this tennis renaissance at the time, the game so far in vogue that it thereby seemed diminished. Women everywhere were acquiring pert, whiter-than-white little outfits and Tretorn shoes and fifty-dollar rackets, even if they didn't yet quite know how to serve or track the score.

That first doubles match quickly belonged to Corinne

and Lela, not that they were winning partners, but that within a few points' time they set the pace and tone of the game. Soon the cheerful, light, good-sport banter of the other women faded in the face of their refusal to contribute. Lela's presence carried the game beyond exercise and sociability, for here was a woman who wanted to win, who would play her damnedest in order to win, who took it for granted that winning mattered. Corinne was intrigued by her cool resolve, set firmly in her jaw and mouth. At the end Lela didn't stay to chat.

"We'll have to play some singles," was all she said, almond eyes averted in quick, downward glances, oddly more piercing than a point-blank stare.

"I met Don Porter's wife today," Corinne told Jack later. "She goes for the ace."

"The one with the hair?" he said.

"Yes," Corinne answered. "The one with the hair. The one with the hair and the apricot MG."

Corinne has group pictures of some of her classes over the years, and she's sure if she can see the boy's face again she'll be able to remember his name. *Victor* sounds like a a distinct possibility, but then so does *Melvin.* She drags one box from the linen closet and starts to rummage through envelopes but can't persist against the heat. The photos feel sticky in her hands, and older ones begin to curl. There's one of Jack as a very young man, barely eighteen in white Navy duds, bleary with beer and raising a mug in some forgotten port of call. She could mail it to him because it's his, but it would only end up with the wife. Light and chemicals combine to freeze up time and sustain it on flimsy scraps of paper. Corinne can barely lift the box to replace it on the shelf. There must be an age past which you stop accumulating baggage, begin to lighten your own load. Maybe Jack has hit it, mailing tennis rackets cross-country without explanatory notes.

She picks up the racket to try a few swings. The grip is much newer than the frame—Jack had it rewrapped for her one year. There is a slight diagonal separation of hide where wood shows through, due less to faulty craftsmanship than to Corinne's habitual twisting of the wrist for extra English on the ball, a quirky movement that worked against the grip. "You have a wickedly controlled slice," Lela told her once, the only compliment Corinne can remember, presuming it was a compliment, since Lela herself liked to hit flat and hard. Corinne sniffs at the leather for mustiness, imagines a faint smell of sweat underneath. Forehand, backhand, pretend a toss and serve. Lift the ball in rhythm with backswing. Release at the maximum height of your arm, hitting the ball at its own high point. Racket forward as if to hurl it over the net, and don't neglect to follow through. An awkwardness registers in her shoulder, not stiffness so much as a forgetting how to move.

Sometimes on the courts in Granite there'd be women actually throwing their rackets over the net by order of instructors. Corinne stubbornly resisted lessons, not wanting to spoil her "natural" game. It was lessons that had turned Don Porter's serve into an elaborate curlicue, worthy of Jacques Tati, as he consciously tried to incorporate the "scratch your back" motion described by pros. Women who had had too many lessons might bounce the ball up to six or eight times, a ritual that drove Corinne crazy in the heat, performed by partner or opponent. Once Lela noticed this, she tried to use it on advantage points, even at the risk of devastating her own service rhythm. The ploy backfired, as it turned out, since by then half of Corinne's pleasure in playing came from watching whatever Lela did and how.

"What's the ultimate in courage?" Don asked her, stoned at the Theobalds', watching Lela dance. "Two cannibals having oral sex."

Corinne hadn't been expecting a joke. "Or mutual trust," she said. "What is the ultimate in mutual trust."

"Don't edit my jokes, woman." Don tried to laugh. "You're picking up terrible manners from my wife."

The first time she met Jack, Lela asked Corinne how old he was, and she had answered automatically, though surprised, even hurt, by the question. No doubt the difference in their ages was often noted or discussed, but never in their presence, apropos of nothing. "How old is Jack, anyway?" Lela said, and with Jack out of earshot, the question diminished them as a couple, seemed to assert their separateness. "He doesn't look it," Lela went on. "He's got the torso of a younger man."

As a midwestern child Corinne watched trains roll into the GM&O station across from her house in Willow, bearing flag-draped coffins from Korea. Hearses would arrive with time to spare and back into a designated spot where mail cars could unload. There would be a small crowd standing quietly at a respectful distance from the soldier's family, and the train when it approached would never clang its bell. Passengers were let off first, before the mail car door slid open, and greetings were subdued and quick. No one would leave before the casket had been eased out onto a baggage cart, wheeled over to the hearse, and lowered in. Sometimes local academy boys turned out in uniform to accomplish this and salute. People might go to their cars then, but no motors were revved before the hearse pulled out and the train slid away. Filled with a dreadful, confused excitement, Corinne would linger on the porch steps until past dark, yearning toward some afterimage to re-animate the desolate parking lot.

While she was watching corpses arrive, Jack was aboard ship in the Pacific, decoding radio messages and waiting for discharge papers or armistice, whichever came first. They had both been shocked to realize this and acknowledge themselves a generation apart. By the time Corinne lay flat out in a Girl Scout tent, listening to Molly McPherson read flashlit scenes from *Peyton Place*, Jack was already married and already wanting out, just waiting, he would later claim, for Corinne to grow up and spring him. He taught her how to suck his cock and sit on his lap for the deepest come. Returning home to her in winter he would nuzzle her neck with a red-gray beardful of snow.

At first they bathed together—the house on Persimmon had a long, old claw-foot tub with curving edges. They'd buy lemon-shaped yellow soap that didn't lather much and leave it to roll about and scent the water. Jack in first and she would lower herself carefully between his legs, lean back against his belly while he splashed and sponged her down the front. Sometimes this would lead them to bed or sometimes it was just a bath—Corinne could wash his cock with the tender efficiency of any nurse or legal whore. Jack soon reverted to showers, but even after many years he would push up his sleeves, kneel beside the tub, and scrub her back until it squeaked. Once after Lela, Corinne heard him sobbing in the basement shower, though he didn't let on when he came upstairs, and she couldn't bear to speak of his pain. Love is so much more scalding and intricate than the infamous sociology of sex. Corinne would rather picture Jack making love to this other wife right now than to think about him bathing her.

The best play is always serious—Jack made them read *Homo Ludens* for class. Serious play is freedom, outside real life into limited time and space, circumstantial order, a definite course. The seductive power of the game is illusion—something real can be decided if the pretense is kept below consciousness. "The play's the thing" is Hamlet, but Corinne remembers the treacherous Iago best. Billie Jean King said she hated to lose more than she ever loved to win.

A sharp, loud jolt through the bedsprings propels Corinne up and running to the narrow bathroom corridor where she feels safest during quakes. By the time she gets there it's already over, but she stands bracing herself anyway, taking a few deliberate breaths, waiting for her heart to slow. They insist temperature is not a factor, but this happens often enough that Angelenos grow uneasy in a heat wave, laughing it off as Shake-and-Bake. Barely a year since Landers-Big Bear, a 7.6 with sixty thousand aftershocks. Probably this is just one more. Out the window nothing appears disturbed, though a car alarm is pointlessly screaming. On TV there is the instant report, 3.8, no damage done.

Corinne lifts her blouse in front of the fan to catch cool air across her breasts. Not cool at all, but stirring at least. Carole King was the rage, and someone kept playing "I Feel the Earth Move" over and over till Corinne finally drank enough to dance, out on a patio, joining Lela, Don still watching from the door. People might have figured they planned the look, wide-sleeved Indian cotton dresses down to the ankle (already so sixties, already passé). Whirling around some poor grad student who naturally thought himself the point. In the Theobalds' bathroom, patchouli and silver eyeshadow, Lela wearing too much of both and then applying more,

garish but entrancing, her lame excuse for following Corinne and locking the door behind them. Lela turns
toward her slightly and says into the mirror, "How much
longer do we have to not kiss?" Electrifying needles
shoot the length of Corinne's spine. Every one-point
jump on the Richter scale means a thirtyfold increase
of energy released.

You may be powerless to do anything except submit, surrender.
Corinne has been toying with the cloth sack of runes,
and STANDSTILL has tumbled out onto the bedspread,
tantamount to drawing it a third time in two days. *What
you are experiencing is the result of conditions of the time, against
which you can do nothing.* Checkmate. Last play in Scrabble
and holding the Z and Q. Caught in no man's land on
Lela's misdirected return.

Patchouli is not a benign fragrance. Lela would dab
it at the base of her throat, but it seemed to permeate
her hair. Incongruous with summer sweat, the scent
would waft across the court to shatter Corinne's concentration. In a crowd now, every once in a while, someone
will wear too much of it, and Corinne can feel desire
rise up, like nausea through pain.

Hit middle age and suddenly your story seems too
long and tortuous to keep straight yourself, much less
convey to someone new. That Tennessee Williams poem
on how people burn to death in hotel rooms: in bed
together, after sex, smoking and failing to stay awake

through each other's autobiographies. Marijuana and incense and patchouli oil, these were olfactory signs of
the times. Jack stoned, too, at the Theobalds' party,
adamant cock the whole drive back, her not wanting
him to touch her and ask what got her wet. At home
bathing quickly, rolling away in bed so he would enter
from the rear. Refusing to kiss him or close her eyes,
when Lela was all there was to see. White heat erupts
unexplained between women, igniting tinder they keep
sealed away. Lela, Lela, Lela, Lela—slow syllabic thrill
on the tongue. Lela and Lela and Lela and Lela, every
measured thrust a cry.

The four of them played doubles once, Don's slow,
clumsy swing and tortured double faults eroding all hope
of compatible rhythms. The Porters' marriage was in
trouble, and you could see it on the court—they had
rarely played as partners and seemed unsure which space
belonged to whom. Several times when Jack or Corinne
put a shot down the middle, they both stood watching
it whiz by, darting each other icy looks. Then they'd
both go for everything, which was nearly as futile, since
it drew them out of position and on return would cost
the point. Even with Lela serving well, Don couldn't
handle the volley at the net—he'd rush forward and
make distracting motions but never simply put away a
shot. Lela would stare at him coldly while he cursed
himself, and soon Corinne and Jack were out of kilter,

too. Don would hang out in alien territory, halfway between the base and service lines, and when he got his racket on a ball, he'd chop it, always to Corinne. Too far back to volley and too close in for a solid ground stroke, she would have to chop in turn, giving Lela her opening to slam it out of play.

"Either move up or back, will you?" Jack finally snapped, though they had yet to lose a game. "You're screwing us up." He rarely gave Corinne instructions on court, both because he didn't need to and because he knew she loathed it. She tried to stay up, which led Don into desperate lobs. The appropriate response would have been to ram the ball back down his throat, but instead Corinne allowed it to bounce, then lobbed it back, offering him a chance to score. It was always Lela who would rush in quickly, call it hers, and aim a brutal overhead smash right into Corinne's feet. "Shit," Jack scolded. "What the hell were you thinking?" The foursome didn't play again.

Don was one of the last men in Granite to cut off his hippie hair, and in the picture Corinne has of him arm-in-arm with Lela, it's their exuberant hair that dominates the frame and makes them look a couple. At home they'd reached an impasse and both gone out on strike—the place cried out to be scrubbed and vacuumed and tidied up. Their house was farther from campus than most faculty lived, hardly more than a bungalow with ugly asphalt siding. Corinne had imagined Lela living in a version of offbeat elegance that did not include gloomy drapes and thin, gray carpeting bedecked with shabby landlord furniture, the kitchen abounding in dirty dishes with trash bags stacked along one wall. From amid the clutter of newspapers, stray plates and ashtrays, Lela would emerge, impeccably dressed, to serve stuffed mushrooms from a highly polished silver tray. When Don moved out, Corinne and Jack helped her paint the whole place lavender and white. Once in a while the three of them would play a set of tennis, Jack holding his own against her and Lela, apex of a triangle that held Corinne in what she mistook for equilibrium.

Pain is information. Corinne was struck by this simple sentence tucked inside an aspirin commercial. Of course, it is basic medical truth, pain designed to alert us to danger and rouse avoidant or curative effort. If pain is information, what passes for love can be very informative, though when pain and pleasure boundaries blur, the warning signs equivocate. Now there are toll-free numbers to call about pain, broadcast in ads during horror shows or colorized romances at 2:00 or 3:00 or 4:00 A.M. Pain Management, Incorporated, is waiting to take your call, and Wound Care Centers of Southern California offer new technology for wounds that will not heal. The American Chronic Pain Association seeks volunteers for self-help groups. Corinne has relished these ads, timed for Fitzgerald's dark night of the soul and seeming to parody Nathanael West. The deepest pain, from internal organs, is felt on the surface, thoroughly displaced. All around a healing wound will swell up what is called *proud flesh*. Be grateful for scars that hold us together.

In the kitchen Corinne uses a table knife to pry a tray from the freezer, where cascades of frost have partly sealed the door. The STANDSTILL rune is labeled ICE/THAT WHICH IMPEDES, possibly profound but as yet unclear to her. It may or may not apply to this old fridge, since of late some puddles have appeared on the floor. She fills a glass with ice cubes, which flavor the water, even more chemical than straight from the tap. It seems now that *Palmer* or *Pierre* might be one of the boy's names. Not *Pierre Palmer* but *Perry*. *Pierre Perry* or *Perry Palmer*. *Montgomery* is the capital of Alabama. But it has to be a two-syllable name. Where would a whole truckful of giant loofah sponges come from? "At least I even got a job," he said. *André* has been a popular one, but *André* is not the name she needs, which almost certainly begins with *M*.

If the brain doesn't know the difference chemically between an actual and imagined experience, she ought to be able to cool herself off by remembering an ice storm. It doesn't work, maybe because the idea is too spectacularly visual, short on touch. What she yearns for, anyway, is rain. She tries to recall the deluge from January, a three-week downpour after years of drought. She lies across the bed, eyes closed, and concentrates on sound and smell. There seems to be no cooling effect, just a kind of dark, humid veil. Houses were sliding down hills in Laguna, and a toilet in Pasadena gushed thousands of gallons of sewage into one woman's home. "Everybody's business from all over town," she said, subdued, on TV news. More information there than anyone required, the mess and then the stench, and how in hell begin to clean?

Jack mostly used the bathroom in the basement, so Corinne had the one upstairs to herself. Some claim such arrangements cause marriages to endure. But it was she who scrubbed the toilets, Jack who earned the money. She washed and ironed and cleaned and shopped and cooked. What can she have cooked, twelve years' worth of meals? Baked potatoes spring to mind. Women with jobs or children would ask her what she did with her time. "Jesus, Corinne," Lela finally said. "What is it that you do all day?"

"I don't know," she answered. "I really don't know what it is I do." By then whatever it was seemed to depend on Lela and Jack, on fitting herself around their bodies and teaching schedules, trying to drink away the guilt and waiting, waiting for Lela to call.

It is difficult for Corinne to hold in mind that she, not Lela, more often won their matches, because, scoring aside, she always considered Lela the superior player, unquestionably the dominant force. Lela played a power game, going for the big serve, the big risk, the big rush, the big slam. When it worked, Corinne was outclassed, but mostly her more measured aim for control and consistency won out, not because that style scored points so much as because Lela's response to it, if not right on the mark, lost points for her. Lela had not yet mastered the game she was striving to play and could therefore defeat herself, becoming angry and disappointed, then going for the power stroke ever more wildly. She could get herself into a downward spiral while Corinne remained calm and collected. Still, Lela was the player with more potential, and in the course of their playing together it was Lela who improved and began to get control of her game, not Corinne who expanded the force of her own.

The most terrifying thing about Lela was simply Corinne's inability to resist her. There was no way to take back the kiss in the Theobalds' bathroom, no way to laugh it off as silly or circumstantial, which perhaps the dancing had been. Certainly not everything erotic had to be overtly sexual. Lela had been a staple of her fantasies for weeks by then, but she had reassured herself that this need have no more relation to outward reality than images of the paperboy, her father's cock, some flagrant bestiality. She spent several days waiting to hear from Lela, imagining they might talk their way out of an untenable situation. But now there was the fact of Lela's tongue, her yearning for that actual tongue, the way it seemed to belong inside her mouth as surely as her own tongue did. Corinne felt defied by gravity, suddenly an unseatable guest in her own home.

She did not call Lela, and Lela, it became apparent,

gave no thought to calling her. They had long since abandoned doubles and opted for a deserted blacktop court near the city golf course, its rough surface and saggy net preferable to sharing game time with other wives reserving college courts. Their regular tennis date came round as if no cataclysm had occurred.

Through epiphanous hindsight Corinne perceives that morning as their defining moment. Not the audacious and steamy scene at the Theobalds', but the dull gray morning several days later when Corinne, who had barely slept or eaten in the interim, arrived at the sunken old court to find Lela, not waiting for her in the MG as usual, but at practice out on the blacktop with a full bucket of balls, totally absorbed in burning them in, following all the way through each time, oblivious to Corinne's presence. Corinne stood on the hill for several minutes watching what became for her an exquisite, solitary dance, as if the motions of tennis had been invented and choreographed solely to exhibit the beauty and grace of Lela's body. All things, surely, were manageable.

The sky was darkening, and Corinne, descending with her racket, thought maybe they wouldn't try to play at all, maybe they would go somewhere public and safe for coffee. "Look out, Wade," Lela called. "This is the day I take you in two quick sets. Before we get rained out." She blew Corinne a cross-court kiss, laughed "love-love" before her serve, and was well on her way to six straight games before raindrops began to splat. The two raced up the hill but were nearly soaked by the time they got the top on the car snapped down. Long breathy silence, then, rackets tucked behind the seats, bare wet thighs on the verge of touch, the muted sound of rain on canvas.

"Well," Lela finally said. "Mother Nature spared you the humiliation." She began to unweave her braid and fluff it out to dry, Corinne trying not to watch.

"We need to talk," she said.

"We do?" Lela held bobby pins with her teeth. "What do we need to talk about?" She reached across Corinne to the glove compartment, tossed in the pins and pulled out a brush. Her strokes were long and slow and efficient, the hair and the motion filling the car. Corinne rolled down her window as far as she could without getting rained on. Golfers across the road were scurrying for shelter. Lela finished her own hair and began on Corinne's pixie, short, light strokes until the space between them could not contain the charge. The kissing was hungry, immediately too much and not enough.

"You're scaring me," Corinne said. "Or I'm scaring myself. This is new for me."

"Two virgins," Lela smirked.

"We need to talk."

"Talk, huh?" Lela teased, leaning back in. "What is there to talk about?"

"There's Jack," Corinne said. "I can't be hurting him with this."

"It has nothing to do with Jack," Lela said. "Does he own you and all your feelings because you're married?

Holy matrimony. It's a farce because it's not realistic. It doesn't allow people to be who they are. This turns out to be who we are. Don't make such a big, heavy deal of it."

At the time this sounded right, at least right enough to rationalize with the sting of desire Corinne could not control. At forty-eight she is relieved (and certain) she will not have to suffer that passion again. The past year with Ginger has been sane and comfortable, affection kept simple, buoyed by physical warmth, a far cry from cunt madness of the sort that Lela inspired. That day in the car was their only attempt ever to analyze what was happening. In law adultery is called *criminal conversation*.

Some distance north you can read the weather by the sun on the HOLLYWOOD sign, not merely the bright white sparkle but the illusive depth of each huge letter, banked against the dark hillside. No clouds, no haze, no fog, no smog—an absence of everything in the atmosphere that obscures or detracts from the wonder of the city. In this neighborhood it's no surprise to see the bed of a pickup on someone's lawn, intact but with no evidence of the truck it once belonged to. There are wrecked and abandoned vehicles, occasionally inhabited. On weekdays certain workmen like to turn off Western or Melrose, park in the shadow of a palm, eat lunch from white sacks in their cars. Sometimes they will take off their shoes, lie back for siesta with feet out a window.

For several weeks last spring Corinne became aware of a daily noontime white-collar rendezvous beneath her window. The woman would arrive and park, the man pulling up across the street and waiting for her to come to him. They might spend an hour there, as passionate as they could be in daylight, fully clothed, inside a car. Often he would drive them somewhere else, maybe a Sunset Boulevard motel. How many two-hour lunches could they get away with, or how many could they stand? It has been weeks now since they've appeared. If Corinne had kept the thing with Lela secret, would it have consumed itself in a matter of months? Out of innocence or guilt, strength or weakness, she could not keep from confessing to Jack and begging his tolerance, if not forgiveness. He must have seen there was no real choice, that Lela already was inside the marriage. Now it sounds like something you read about in foreign movies, too risky for the Hollywood kind, though, absurdly, East Hollywood is where Corinne has ended up. Today the skies above the sign look as pure as those over Granite, laid out flat amid the tallest corn of central Illinois.

Lela and Don were both from Chicago and held downstate in customary contempt, so it surprised Corinne and Jack to run into them at the corn festival that year, late in August, on the courthouse square. This was not an event many university people attended, but

Corinne always wanted to go. Thinking of it now, in fact, inspires outright nostalgia, the air heavy and sweet with the fragrance of boiling corn, steamy trash barrels full of husks, warm bread pans brimming with melted butter. The streets between the courthouse and surrounding storefronts would be lined with red-checkered tables arrayed with one-pound boxes of salt and enormous glass pitchers of ice-cold tea.

Suddenly there was Lela in her silky white sundress, the one with bold blue flowers that on a hanger would not have called for a second glance. Suddenly there was the odor of patchouli and Lela, strolling apart from Don, gazing across the tables into the window of Egger's Department Store, looking as if she might angle over and window-shop in earnest. Right at the sunlit center of truckloads of fresh-picked corn, a concentration of patchouli oil, evoking closed-in rooms, candlelight, Indian bedspreads, rumpled sheets. And there were Lela's breasts, situated so perfectly inside the shapeless dress they made it look well cut. Later at a table, the four of them chatting and gnawing corn, Corinne began to stare at the thin white strings that held up the dress—the flimsy bows on each shoulder that seemed to loosen more each time Lela's hair, in her turning, caressed them. Soon the bold blue flowers slipped, carelessly revealing cleavage. Corinne saw Jack was watching too. Finally she whispered, behind her hand, "I think your straps are coming down."

"Oh, thanks," Lela said, but she made no move to secure them.

Corinne herself would not have worn such a dress, but if she had she'd have tied knots in the strings before tying bows. She tried to stop watching Lela and keep her eye on Jack. Ordinarily it would have been something to tease him over later, but she already knew she wouldn't, even though this was early on, when nothing among them had gone beyond tennis. Don was sporting a T-shirt with the cartoon of a very pregnant Mona Lisa saying NIXON'S THE ONE, deliberately drawing looks of disapproval from solid Republican townsfolk in the midst of Watergate. The mixed doubles must have been Don's idea. That same fall Billie Jean King trounced Bobby Riggs, which underneath the hoopla felt like a serious victory.

Billie Jean was always a thrill, the embodiment of passion and power, rushing the net ferociously, pushing her whole soul into the ball. She was noisy on court but spontaneously so, out of exasperation or effort. Bent deep at the knee she'd be ready to spring with barely the patience to wait for a bounce. Now it's Monica Seles and Steffi Graf, such excellent tennis, a yawn to watch. It's Seles with her bisyllabic grunt, annoyingly sexual in its vulgar automation, Graf pale and spiritless and silently efficient. Corinne caught the last Virginia Slims on TV and felt quite keenly old, a puffy Billie Jean in the stands watching Seles beat Navratilova, who's exactly twice her age. "Chrissie Evert is a wife and

mother," the announcer cooed, "and Martina's still playing at a young thirty-six." King's been coaching Martina,
who's fading fast, and when she goes there'll be no one
to watch. The day of the finals was Billie Jean's birthday.
Corinne had forgotten they were born the same year,
though she did recall they married six months apart.

Maybe there's nothing so exciting as an outright tomboy on court. Seeing a sedentary King made Corinne
long for the old fire and spunk. "I don't care if he comes
out wearing a jockstrap," she said of Riggs, and pro-
ceeded to whip him back and forth along the baseline
as if her life hung on every point. The night of the
match Lela came directly home from a meeting at her
school and bet her entire paycheck on King in straight
sets, winning six hundred dollars from the flabbergasted
men in the room, including Jack and Don. Corinne
stood in awe of this, having no money of her own to
bet. It made King's triumph all the more delicious,
though Corinne and Lela later joked no woman in
America got laid that night.

Corinne has ceased to speculate on why it was L.A.
she fled to, though once the triangle collapsed on her,
midwestern winters grew extreme. People love to tell
stories of rats in the palm trees, an unacknowledged
metaphor of personal disappointment. They migrate
here with vain expectations, then feel betrayed that the
palms were shipped in, too. *I'd be safe and warm if I was
in L.A.* Now it's known as the Calamity Capital of the
World. Here you lose yourself or find yourself in

crowded, open spaces—the most complex and precarious of towns.

When she first got settled and realized that tennis was possible all year round, Corinne aspired to a fresh take on the game, some way to reclaim it for herself. She met a man who said he played, on scheduled time at La Cienega Courts. An affable sort, he brought fluorescent orange balls and played as if long rallies were the object of the sport. Tennis to him meant exercise and sunshine, a healthy attitude, Corinne was half convinced. But each time they met, her strokes grew less focused, and she'd start to tire halfway through a set. Her racket became almost too burdensome to grip, those gaudy balls registering as if they were waterlogged. The effort involved seemed silly and pointless when whatever-his-name-was was having such fun. There was really nothing wrong with the man except that he wasn't Jack. At rest on a side bench, he kissed her cheek and offered a massage, and Corinne saw that tennis would be as irretrievable as the marriage. She covered the racket and put it away and hasn't yet been back on court.

Those tiny-faced, nearly round steel rackets. Mostly handle, no need for a press. Their heyday was brief as wood went out but before the composites became de rigueur. Hers is in the living room closet, she knows, since it fell from a shelf some months ago. Corinne gets it out, unsheathes it, and stands it next to the Little Mo. A Wilson T2000, made in the USA. At the butt of the grip, etched onto white, a large red *W* rivets the eye.

She and Lela would spin and let it drop, call it up or down to determine first serve. Really Corinne preferred that Lela go first, so she could work under pressure to hold her own. Billie Jean and Margaret Court played two sets forever one Wimbledon, forty-six protracted games, running the TV lineup amuck. These days tiebreakers force a winner quick. Tennis, that most peculiar sport, where it's possible to score more points than your opponent and still end up losing the match.

Donovan, the man's name was, Russell Donovan, an underwriter, which Corinne considered an amusing word if not an amusing occupation. *Underwriter, undertaker, underdog.* There is a word for the kind of legs Lela had, flat and straight down the back, but it is a word Corinne just barely ever knew, and she holds no hope of recollecting it now, unless it is simply, unaesthetically, *hyperflexed*, which she's fairly certain it is not. Lela all heat and chill on court or off, simultaneous fire and ice, wine-dark nipples sucked up beyond pleasure, Corinne drunk on the taste of her cunt. "What is your stereotype, Ms. Wade?" The boy's a man now, full-grown cock.

Jack driving home through sleet from the Goodwill store, the perfect chair for fucking tied atop the car. High-backed, dull green and velvet soft, its narrow seat was cushioned, unimpeded by arms. He set it before her in the dining room, no explanation required. For years a sidelong glance its way brought her naked like magic onto his lap. They'd smile like conspirators if a guest sat in that chair, unless the guest was Lela, which they would both ignore. What if the three of them had gone ahead, what if they had had the nerve? Corinne has mulled this over and over, how it might have worked out if either she'd kept Lela entirely to herself or guided them all to an outright ménage. In dreams she's still the one who gets to have Jack inside her, whatever Lela does in shadow or in harsh white light.

Corinne has been lying face down on the bed, crunching shards of bitter ice. Now she sits up against thick pillows and fishes the last two dripping cubes from the glass, one for each nipple up under her shirt. Cold shock passes quickly, sharp burn to ache, before the stiffened flesh grows numb. She slips one hand inside her skirt, one icy finger straight to the clit. If she can't make him read, she can teach him how to fuck her, show her what's not on TV. Unzip and pull it and sit on him hard. Steps off the truck. Coal skin glistens. Jack and jack and jack him away.

She awakes with a headache from the heat, uncomfortably twisted in sweaty clothes. She carries the fan to the bathroom doorway, strips and runs the tub three-quarters full of lukewarm water. Life's most benign and dependable, transformative pleasure. White birch-and-almond gel will camouflage the chlorine, enabling her to luxuriate in hydro-aromatherapy. The tub is not quite long enough to sink to her chin and stretch out flat—she has to situate herself with an awkward bend at the knee. Oddly angled and seen through water, folds of flesh are magnified. Too thick at the waist now for decent tennis, even if the legs and wrist held out. Corinne's self-styled, natural game depended on the energetic rhythm of youth.

The boy's name is *Malcolm*, absolutely, it rises across her vision like a bird taking wing. He missed a lot of school, excused by his mother's illness, and was surprised once, but cooperative, when Corinne insisted he make up time. After school in an empty classroom, he sat formally in his regular back-row seat till she coaxed him up front and worked alongside him. Such a struggle to make sense of words, such gentle, hesitant delight when he could. He never seemed to fit in his body, overgrown with an oddly feminine cast. Great big feet and rounded hips. How could she forget his name, with the flaming X across his chest? But ubiquitous symbols lose their jolt, and X suggests every undesignated variable. It's possible now to go to the store and forget items written on the list in her hand.

Corinne jerks suddenly in the water, unsure if there's been a second tremor. Bathtub tsunami. She stretches her legs, bracing them against blue tile above the faucets. Scorching soles on summer asphalt, her flattening feet would never hold up. Too many quick starts and stops in tennis, though the shoes now result from elaborate technology. Jack thrilled his students with enlightening questions rather than useful information. She stares at her ankles, where lately tiny veins are breaking.

Does LIESTILL deserve a separate rune? Framed from the other side of the wall, she would have to be foreshortened. Probably she should make dinner for Ginger, but nothing holds appeal against the heat. Frozen yogurt. Salad and bread. Maybe an air-conditioned double feature.

Jack never cared if they missed a few scenes, but Corinne still refuses to enter movies late. Trains ran right through the center of town, and an endless freight could make you late for the seven o'clock if you forgot to start early and detour under the viaduct. The house on Persimmon was just up from the tracks, and sometimes Granite's version of a traffic jam would back right up to their front porch, couples in cars anxious and impatient, hoping the previews would outlast the train. Jack on the glider reading the local paper, Corinne stretched out with her head in his lap. She loved to watch rain blow against the screens, filling up patches of tiny squares. Jack would read the paper aloud and pet her like a cat. Sometimes she would sit two steps above him on the basement stairs and watch him shine shoes with literal Navy spit and polish, the tender spot at the back of his neck begging to be softly kissed. At age eleven, on the morning of his Lutheran confirmation, Jack scrubbed his ears until they bled. Crisp button-downs in plastic lying flat across the car seat. Toward the end they'd bump into each other in doorways and swear. Corinne pulls the plug with her toe and watches water seep slowly away beneath her.

Lela's feet were vulgar, in startling contrast to her ankles and legs. Square, bony feet, more suited to one of Van Gogh's toiling peasants than to Lela, who pretended to be self-conscious about them but went barefoot a lot, even in winter. "Don't be looking at my feet," she said once. "They're ugly. Ignore them."

Corinne had to laugh, since indeed they were ugly. "They're not ugly," she said. "They're perfectly good feet."

But Corinne did examine them every chance she got. Lela was so adept at masking vulnerability that her softness finally came to reside in those knotty, indelicate feet. Meeting her for wintry breakfasts at the Illini House Coffeeshop, Corinne would get there early so she could watch Lela enter the room, the way heads would turn for a woman that tall who knew how to walk in a pair of boots. Lela the X factor, solidly planted on those tender, virile feet.

At the mirror Corinne kneads her short, momentarily damp hair in a futile attempt to reinspire some curl. A chemical quirk or blow to the head can cause *agnosia*, your own reflection or photograph a sudden stranger to your brain. Orwell said at fifty the face we have is the face we deserve, and Corinne thinks he was probably right, at least under normal circumstance, if such a thing can be defined. She sees strength in her face, she hopes not hardness. A good mouth-fuck, you can see it in the thickness and set of her lips. Once Jack surprised her with brandy on his cock, and she loved his knowing to do it just once. He liked her kneeling in front of the closet mirror, both under the spell until there was no delineation of pleasure between the doing and the watching do. Her green eyes seem to be darkening with age, sandy hair not graying but fading nonetheless. Rejecting underwear she slips into thin khaki pants and a white sleeveless top, both warm enough against her skin to have come straight from the dryer.

Corinne can remember late-night TV alone, Jack, thank God, upstairs asleep for Dick Cavett's snide but coyly delivered line: "If your wife is leaving you for another woman, do you have to hold the door for them both?" Her husband took his shirts to be laundered because he knew she hated ironing them, not because she had so much else to do. By the time you comprehend the zeitgeist, it's always too far past to redeem. The way it's too damn hot these days to drive to the beach, where you might cool off.

The old black VW had levered vents that sucked in heat off the engine. Corinne would be halfway to Lela's those deep winter mornings before any warmth at all hit the car. She'd send Jack off walking to class with a kiss, then hasten to make the crosstown drive, sometimes forced to greet Don with mutual honks and waves as he made his way to the university, too. Corinne would arrive dressed in so many layers that stripping down for Lela turned into comic shtick. The scheduling, to be sure, contained elements of farce, but Corinne took the pleasure as seriously as the pain and guilt. "Lighten up" became Lela's refrain.

Corinne had to get there by nine if they were to have a full two hours, since at eleven, somewhere in the afterglow, Lela would turn cool and withdraw and begin methodical preparations to go take charge of a roomful of four- and five-year-olds at Granite's only "alternative" school. Corinne would wrap herself in the bright yellow comforter that Lela used to make the bed less Don's, then watch the transformation from Amazonian nude into bohemian schoolmarm. At the last possible moment Corinne would jump up quickly and into her own disarray of clothing so they could exit the house together, into a white frosted sparkle of sun keen enough to make them both tear up and sneeze. On slightly warmer days, with studied aplomb, Lela would unsnap the top of the MG and speed off hatless into her day, Corinne unable to catch her or even keep her in sight for long.

At one-fifteen at least three days a week Jack would come home for a lunch hour that stretched into long afternoons upstairs. Corinne would get in from Lela's with just enough time to bathe and re-dress and deal with the food, sipping rosé to smooth the transition. Lunch and wine and up to bed, Jack more fierce than tender or playful, just the way she wanted him then. If half her excitement was left over from the morning, Jack soon claimed it for his own, thrusting fast and deep past Lela, no doubt his inspired intent. Corinne gave into them both with cumulative appreciation and as much abandon as possible under the rigid structure of circumstance. There is power in making a woman come, more alluring and mysterious than the predictable, automatic male crescendo. Sometimes with Lela she'd become aware of Jack, standing beside the bed and watching, waiting, fully erect. That period of weeks blurred itself from erotic frenzy to erotic stupor, concentrated devotion to the art of sexual intensity. And Corinne came to believe that this was why she existed, what she was made to do on Earth. Now she's amazed at her stamina and all the baths—at least two midwinter baths a day, dreadfully parching her skin, however much lotion she tried to lather on. Dressing, undressing, dressing again; undressing, dressing, undressing again; then dressing for evening, undressing to sleep.

Logistics could not support that pace, of course. Somebody had a schedule change, somebody got tired or sick, somebody's libido waned. Lela started playing occasional morning tennis at the Racquet Club with a lawyer whose wife was on the board of her school. Soon after that, before spring quarter, Don resigned his job and took off for Colorado. Corinne and Jack were present the night that marriage cracked for good, the four of them out for dinner at Taylor's Steakhouse, drinking too many martinis before getting a booth. Suddenly Lela was saying, "One of us needs to look for another place," and Don was nodding but looked as if he'd been struck in the face, the moment more intimate and terrible to witness than if they had actually come to blows. Firmly etched in Corinne's mind is the hostess screeching over and over at the mike, "Ledbetter, Ledbetter, party of ten." Very soon after Don's departure, the triangle closed as if it had never been a square. If Lela did any grieving, she kept it to herself. "I'm going to clean this place up, finally," she said, standing amid boxes of books and records ready to be shipped west. "Throw out this crappy carpet. Get some big plants in here. And let's paint everything purple. Why not?" Jack in tight-fitting, spattered sweats, dragging her mattress back to its spot on the bedroom floor. Lela watches him from the doorway in a baggy old white shirt of Don's, a thick smear of lavender all down one sleeve. Soon Lela will be included in all their plans, though they will not be included in hers. Corinne fared best when the three of them were together—the more it appeared Jack liked and accepted Lela, the safer and saner Corinne felt. She took Lela's outspoken contempt for marriage as posturing, an attempt to rationalize her impending divorce, and she was shocked when she realized Lela must be screwing Sam Gorman in addition to beating him at tennis.

"I wish you could see it," she told Corinne. "I take both sets. I think he's uptight about being seen with me at the club. I think I intimidate him, anyway. It's downright funny, really. I cream him almost every game."

"Cream his jeans, anyway." Corinne said this as lightly as possible, though jealous outrage clutched her heart so tight she could barely take a normal breath.

"Cute," Lela said. "Cream his jeans."

"What about Miriam?"

"Miriam doesn't play." Lela kept on smiling. "What can I tell you?"

Jack would ask, "Do you think Lela's all right over there? It must be tough for a woman alone. Sometimes she seems to look so sad."

"She's all right," Corinne assured him. "I wouldn't be all right. But Lela's all right."

What you want is to meet the ball at the center of the racket. You want to focus on the ball, not merely on the ball but on the seams of the ball, as it heads your way. You want to watch the ball from the moment it leaves your opponent's racket until the moment it hits yours. You want to watch the ball until you see it is actually larger than you thought, that it actually moves more slowly as it approaches you. You want to watch the seams of the ball hit not the exact center of your racket, but one inch below where the center would be. And then you want to listen to the ball. You want to hear the ball make that perfectly resonant, solid *thunk* that means you've done it right. You want your mind so occupied with that incoming ball that your body forgets to try too hard, your body is free to make the automatic moves that will get it where it needs to be, racket extended exactly so far, waiting to hear that sweet-spot sound. You want to allow yourself to execute this perfectly, stretching along the here and now. The task, after all, is exquisitely simple: Hit it over the net and into the opposite court. Over the net, inside the lines, and out of your designated enemy's control. You want the rhythm in your bones, you want momentum on your side. You want every shot to be a sweet-spot shot, which every shot will never be.

Still the sweet spot seems to splinter first, in a sad expenditure of dignity. These old wooden rackets are museum pieces now. Probably no one restrings them anymore. Corinne stands, racket to belly, poised at the center of her bedroom, plucking the "Duelling Banjos" theme. It was Eric Berne who pinpointed games as based on ulterior motives. Interior, exterior, ulterior. Slamming the ball directly into the center of Lela's back. Notches can't be carved so easily into steel.

You may be experiencing an unaccustomed drain on your energy and wonder why. Do not hope to rely on help or friendly support. Halfway downstairs Corinne regrets she is barefoot, grit from the fraying carpet setting her teeth on edge. The check is there, nothing else, and she has to admit disappointment, as if yesterday's extraordinary package should bode another marvel today. For years she received periodic notes from Don in Boulder, which she answered with such reluctance that he finally gave up. Curious, to hear from him like that, when she so seldom heard from Jack and only once from Lela, a card with no return address, postmarked Washington, D.C. She fights the impulse to recheck the mailbox, the absurd idea Jack's letter is somehow stuck at the top of the slot. There was a wild passionflower vine that spread itself across the evergreen hedge beneath their dining room window, intricate purple-fringed blossoms popping open in time-lapse time. Such exotic, delicate plants to survive harsh winters, even to thrive on cold neglect.

This joblessness has overstayed its welcome. Corinne could twist herself into panic with very little effort, though at times she envies bag ladies their unencumbered lives. "Irregular" employees may not hear before July. She ought to go get certified for teaching ESL. Lately Corinne is miserable in the apartment but oddly reluctant to leave it, disinclined to test her uneasiness against the outside world. The bank can wait for her check one more day. She will use body English to get it there.

Certain normal-looking people with a glitch in serotonin become obsessed and tortured by their own imagined ugliness. They stay in the house and avoid the mirror or keep a constant vigil there. Hide out long enough and you'll get suicidal, especially if you believe your looks will frighten people on the street. They say this is merely seepage, molecules from one neuron exciting another, triggering signals that tell us God-knows-what. *Ledbetter, Ledbetter, party of ten.* What if your neurotransmitters happen to signal you're drop-dead gorgeous? Plain Jane glances into the mirror, suddenly enchanted. Dickinson pictured martyrs for beauty sharing a tomb with those for truth. On the third-floor landing Corinne turns and redescends. She thinks it can't hurt all that much to double-check the mail.

Lela in pale green slacks and a pale rose scoop-neck sweater is plaiting a darker rose-colored scarf into a belt, the crucial adornment that will create the defining impression, not logical in the least, that if you just unfasten the right knot or button, everything will come undone and slip down. Lela, constantly willing to leave so much unspoken, beguiling by what she neglects to do or say. She could make Corinne feel there was some secret at her center, a secret Corinne might discover if only she played things right. The silent, seductive promise was that sex would inspire revelation, though in fact the allure dictated revelation could never occur.

At the height of arousal sometimes Lela would look at her direct, and it would be that look, a kind of hypnotic darkening in Lela's eyes, that would edge Corinne up to ecstatic release. For her own pleasure Lela kept her eyes shut, declaring everything in movement and sound, rising finally to sharp, loud cries. She would nestle then against Corinne's breasts and not look up until she'd recomposed herself. They would eat toast or coffee cake and chat in a leisurely way at the bare oak table, keyed to the rhythms that beat beneath words rather than to the words themselves. Between them everything felt like foreplay, never normal conversation. Even afterplay felt like foreplay, so unless Jack was with them, there was no pretense to ordinary friendship.

If he avoided the subject of where Corinne spent her mornings, he never tried to avoid Lela herself. It was Jack who asked if Lela would come along for the movie, meet them at the restaurant, drive to the country for firewood. The three spent several Saturdays scouting indoor auctions in search of items for Lela's house, hauling furniture on top of the Bug, debating paints or strip-and-refinish techniques. Sometimes Corinne or Jack would RSVP parties with an indication that Lela Porter "might be coming along," and eventually people greeting them alone would ask outright where she was. Still Corinne never felt they were viewed with suspicion—it was kind, after all, to extend goodwill to a deserted wife. At the end of the evening, wherever they were, whatever they had done, there always came that wrenching moment when Lela left them or they left her, that moment when Corinne, involuntarily, would begin to mark the time apart. At some point Lela accused Corinne of wanting to possess her, just when Corinne herself was feeling most possessed.

At Scrabble it was Lela who kept meticulous score. Jack defeated himself by arranging unlikely words on his wooden tray and waiting for an opportunity to lay them down. This stubborn illogic allowed Corinne and Lela to triple his score with simple, unimaginative plays. Jack was outraged that his strategy failed and he was forced to sacrifice letters and points to the momentum of the game. "One more letter, I'd have had *pentimento*," he'd say, managing to whine and brag at once. "I get a good shot, you two jump in to mess me up."

"Not our fault," Lela said, "that you consciously choose to sabotage yourself." But Lela liked the words Jack almost made as much as Corinne did. And it was obvious that without him there'd have been no game at all.

"Lela's the only one staying in practice for tennis." Corinne at times couldn't resist this needling. "She's getting spoiled by climate control at the Racquet Club."

"It's true," Lela laughed, taking it well. "You won't have a snowball's chance in hell this spring."

"Who's the guy out there?" Jack wanted to know. "This Gorman guy. Who is he?"

"Just a guy," Lela said, but teasing with her eyes. "Just a local lawyer kind of guy."

"He's married," Corinne added quickly. She saw the relief she expected to see spread across her husband's face.

"The balls are faster on those indoor courts," Lela said. "And you get a nosebleed from sucking dry air."

Lela leaving the house, giving them both small pecks on the cheek. They snap on the back porch light and stand together, watching her move across the yard, watching taillights disappear down the alley. They hold each other for a moment before they go back inside and start turning on lamps, every single downstairs light. The house by then was constantly full, of Lela's presence or Lela's absence—either a lovely, large bouquet or its empty vase deprived of purpose. *Possession,* some say, is nine-tenths of the law.

The carpet is littered with bits of rubbery plastic off the top of the steel racket, laced to protect court surfaces if not the racket itself. The stuff has hardened and crumbled with age. Jack liked to vacuum, made it seem a manly job with his casual, one-handed moving of furniture. Summer evenings the *whir* and *click* of his hand-mower blades brought out the fireflies. That spring before Corinne finally left, the storm windows never got taken down. The upper rim of the wooden racket is flat and smooth, worn past all sign of varnish and paint. The minister who married them hadn't approved of the difference in age or the recent divorce. Jack had to go into the church office for a private and humbling man-to-man. *Forsaking all others, to love and to cherish, death do you part, no man put asunder.* Jack had no strictly social smile, just one for pleasure, one for amusement. His upper teeth were flawlessly straight, the softest of lips against her throat. The thick, flat box he mailed the racket in looks expressly designed for its task. Corinne stares at the wide calligraphic lettering. Her name still his name, no return address.

She will have to buy sponges for soaking up puddles in the kitchen. Corinne layers paper toweling in front of the fridge and then stands debating whether to defrost, certainly, at least, the coolest job in sight. To drink there's beer or the raspberry ginger ale she keeps forgetting to return, presuming the store will let her exchange the six-pack that remains intact. Surely a misguided marketing ploy, to take the only soft drink with any pretense to class and obfuscate it with pink perfume. Maybe she should make herself drink it all as penance for her absent mind. Now that tapes are becoming obsolete, she buys cheap music she wouldn't have before. Pleased to find Steely Dan in the deep-discount bin, she bought *Katy Lied* two weeks in a row. One more item to try to exchange. It may be time to start a list.

"You're just running old tapes in your head," a therapist once scolded. Corinne was paying him to say such things. Consider the brain as a question-and-answer machine. Analyze all transactions. If she does defrost today, the old Hotpoint may never cool back down. Corinne compromises, using a spatula to scrape loose freezer ice into the empty meat tray below, nearly enough to fill the sink, a pure and soothing mountain of white. Nipples rise to attention as she pats it into a solid pyramid. Is this reaction real or memorized? Who first ever thought to say "snowball's chance in hell"?

Corinne has fished Lela's postcard from the rear of her winter sweater drawer, still in its pale yellow frame from years ago when she kept it on display for a while. The image continues to mesmerize: Lartigue's black and white of Suzanne Lenglen caught midair en route to a backhand. She appears to be flying, legs stretched out for the widest possible stride, racket arm extended all the way forward, poised to meet the oncoming ball where her concentration focuses. It's 1921 France, and there is a suggestion of the flapper in the hang of her skirt, the unyielding waistline bow in back, the metallic double bracelets on her upper arm. She is wearing a wide, dark headband, very nearly a hat, and one palm frond from a background tree at first glance passes for extravagant plumage. The wooden racket, under guidance from a bandaged thumb, is held in almost perfect profile, its perpendicular shadow as shortened as that of Lenglen's body is elongated, both beyond recognizable human or objective form. The shoes are shockingly flimsy, secured by ballet strings about the ankles. If you look carefully, you can see that her white stockings stop just above the kneecap, rolled over there and held by elastic garters. The way her left elbow appears to rest upon her thigh in flight anchors the photo and removes any doubt that Lenglen will pull off this bodacious and spectacular shot—the woman after all did nail five Wimbledons in a row. But what strikes Corinne now is the profound air of solitude that emanates from the picture, the unadulterated, poignant force of a player frozen in isolation.

Corrie this made me think of you love Lela. No need to remove the card from its frame to read the message. Corinne knows the words and the way they're laid out, unpunctuated and run together, capitals only on the names. Besides, something in her chest recoils at the

thought of confronting Lela's actual signature. The ges-
ture of the card was characteristically semisweet, Lela
not being a woman inclined to sweetness, nor is Corinne
herself, in fact. If anyone, Jack had the corner on sweet.
Jack would hand Lela a fresh can of balls, even if they
weren't about to play, because he knew she got a kick
from the opening *hiss*. Jack would go out after dark and
rake up leaves for the fireplace if Corinne said she felt
like smelling them burn. *Bittersweet* is named for roots
that start out bitter but sweeten as you chew. So how do
you tell the poisonous kind? *Deadly nightshade,* the hypnotic
belladonna. Corinne reburies the postcard among insulated
garments she rarely wears. The STANDSTILL rune says that
holding on results in a shallowness of feeling. *Lela* is a Per-
sian word for woman born of night.

It's true there was something in Lela that Corinne
yearned to possess: the fearless way she drove a car, for
example, her unguarded delight at speeding up on
curves. She would downshift rather than brake on hills
and loved to scatter gravel in quick reverse. What would
have seemed rude or silly in a teenage boy, in Lela
struck Corinne with the thrill of derring-do. Always ten-
tative behind the wheel herself, she had to marvel at
Lela in charge of the MG—you could feel it responding,
hugging the road, roaring and vibrating beneath the
low-slung seats.

Over time it became apparent that if there was driving

to be done, Lela preferred to do it. Rarely did Corinne, or even Don, drive her anywhere, and eventually, when it got to be Lela and Corinne and Jack, Lela would often drive their VW, with Jack beside her and Corinne in back. Corinne not only submitted to this arrangement but preferred it, savoring the backs of her lovers' heads, tuning in and out of their conversation, immersing herself in a complicated resonance. At times she felt deep relief that Jack and Lela were engaged with each other, expecting nothing from her but silent assent. This was a peculiar, almost eerie, respite, but from what Corinne could never be sure. Once Lela opted out, it was as if Corinne and Jack had lost their navigator. They'd walk to a movie or skip a trip downtown rather than quibble over who should drive.

After Sam Gorman entered the picture, encroaching on Corinne's mornings, she began to humiliate herself once or twice a week by tooling all over Granite in search of Lela's MG or his silver Mercedes. On these anguishing drives she did resort to gunning her motor, did haphazardly screech her brakes. Peeling out in parking lots was less an awkward attempt at style than a nauseous failure to contain her rage. The Beetle must have cut a ridiculous figure eight, from the Racquet Club to the Illini House, then out by the Quality Motor Inn, and back, most desperately, to Lela's driveway. Difficult to say which proved more painful, finding the vehicles snuggled together or not being able to find them at all.

The nadir came one morning at the Racquet Club

when she saw Gorman, then Lela, exit a side court door, him dressed for the office, her for school. The MG was nowhere in sight, and Lela strode directly to the Mercedes, stashed her tennis gear in back, and slid behind the wheel as Gorman looked on, standing motionless, empty-handed, apparently bemused. It seemed to Corinne that he carried himself like a much more handsome man than he was, perhaps the effect of expensive clothes. At least he wasn't female, a chilly comfort that Corinne fervently embraced. She sat observing them, listening to her heart bang, pretending to be invisible in a bright red car across a narrow, unpaved road. Gorman didn't join Lela till she had backed up and circled the club's exit drive, acting as if she'd prefer to leave him stranded. Corinne couldn't bring herself to follow them, but soon the shiny silver coupe was conspicuous in front of the coffeeshop downtown. Corinne got as far as the candy display at the register inside the door. "Look who's here," she would say nonchalantly. "How's the game between you two these days?" Instead she bought Milk Duds to chew in the car, which only made her sicker than she already felt. After that she managed to keep herself at home on the mornings when Lela was occupied.

Mostly Corinne tried not to call her, tried not to keep track in the regular way. This meant she spent much time and energy pretending not to listen for the phone. She began sleeping late, then sleeping later, not exactly sleeping but not exactly getting up and dressed before noon, either. On those days Corinne looked forward to Jack coming home more out of desire to fill the afternoon than out of desire for him. Soon he sensed as much. Things cooled off in bed as suddenly as they had heated up, and he began to spend more time at school.

One morning Corinne arrived as scheduled at Lela's, rang the back bell and got no answer, although the MG was in the garage. She knocked and waited and knocked again, finally going round to the front porch. Through the storm door she saw Lela asleep among pillows on the sofa, lying on her side and half uncovered, one breast, one arm, one calf and foot exposed, a heavy purple bedspread and lavender sheet held snug between her thighs. Her hair lay bunched beneath one cheek, mostly against the pillow, a few strands twisted about her throat in an oddly tender arrangement. The women never fell asleep together, and Corinne resolved to preserve this image, the way Lela's lips were slightly parted, the way her jawline and brow had relaxed, softening her face, nothing in it contrived or defended or set. As she was about to tap the glass, Lela stirred, opening her eyes and jerking the covers up, then gazing at Corinne for a long, unsmiling moment before getting up and striding naked not to the door but all the way back to the bedroom. She returned not in a robe but fully dressed, including boots, fully dressed and fully displeased.

"How long had you been watching me?"

"Maybe a minute," Corinne said. "You make it sound like you caught a Peeping Tom."

"A full minute? You stood there watching me for a whole minute? God. I hate that."

"You should keep your curtains closed," Corinne said.

"Just because the curtains were open doesn't mean you have to stand there staring in. Why didn't you knock? No wonder I can't get any sleep."

"Is it better on the couch?" Corinne said. "Maybe you're missing Don. Maybe you miss having someone here. Maybe it's a big adjustment, even if it's what you wanted."

"I like living alone," Lela said, emphasizing each word separately. "You can't seem to get that straight. Don used to wake me up staring, too. He knew I couldn't stand it."

"Seems like a natural thing to do," Corinne said. "Jack and I do it all the time."

"God, you two," Lela said. "I bet you do. You two really inspire claustrophobia."

"Claustrophobia?" Corinne was stung.

"I'm sorry," Lela said. "Really, I am. It's just that I think the way you live is out of touch with the way things are."

Corinne lacked the courage to ask how things were.

Just as most people turned to steel and aluminum, Jack bought himself a new wooden racket, a handsome black-and-tan model with catgut strings that threatened to stretch at the hint of rain. It's sentimental to judge metal rackets soulless, but still, the wooden ones at least were once alive. The Little Mo, standing head-up now in a sunlit corner of the living room, draws Corinne's eye again and again, beckoning to be held. The T2000 coarsens the room, deserves its cracked plastic cover, seems to belong to someone else or to no one in particular. Tennis is a game of errors in which you score from opponents' mistakes. One cardinal rule: Don't let them know they've hurt you—maintain poise and cover the court. The drop shot is arrhythmic, demeaning, diabolical. When all else fails, you lob for breathing space. Consider the pure mechanics of topspin. Consider the concept of negative lift. Consider winning by attrition. Those wide-body graphites surely dwarf the ball. Corinne never had the least desire to hit two-handed backhands like Chris Evert Lloyd.

One afternoon Jack went to observe Lela teach and came home convinced he should abandon academe and open a preschool himself. It was difficult to tell at first whether this fervor signaled an impending midlife crisis or the intellectualization of his enchantment with Lela. In any case, the three of them were to spend many an evening perfecting the design for this ideal school (hats off to Montessori, salute to A. S. Neill). Corinne's enthusiasm for these discussions had less to do with education than her relief that she and Jack and Lela could conjure a future together at all: Such talk seemed to strengthen the base of the triangle, help choreograph the *pas de trois.* It was Jack's gift for creative optimism that kept him a dedicated teacher and younger than his years. After Lela moved to Baltimore, Corinne and Jack for a time would get brutally stoned on their neighbors' homegrown pot. Corinne once sat cross-legged on the floor in front of Jack, hallucinating fast-forward the aging of his face. This ought to have been an interesting trip, but his thinning hair and slackening jaw had so frightened and saddened her that she couldn't explain why she was crying or why she insisted, that very instant, on serving dinner to bring them down. Now she can't imagine what Jack might look like, though police computers can age photographic images to compensate the years since someone was last seen. Sontag called photos memento mori, hard evidence for the relentless melt of time.

Another mild but definite tremor sends Corinne rushing to the hallway again, but the rumble stops while she's still en route. She lingers at one end of the narrow passage, aiming to calm herself. Instead she envisions being crushed between the two solid walls. Where you choose to hide can kill you. She fights the urge to dash outside, crawls instead beneath the dining room table.

Where was Malcolm during the riot? Probably reading it on TV. He is not the looting type, but what about the civil war? Rodney King, too big and black: cruelly beaten, hurled into history, still nobody's hero. People so stunned by the videotape, it was actually used to acquit the police. Fumes filled the apartment as the fires moved north on Western. What is your stereotype, Ms. Wade? *Each one teach one.* If you can reach one. The children are hooked on stereophonics. If cells can't distinguish imagining from doing, she ought to feel as if she's had the boy, showing up to distract her from Jack, too shallow a come to fool anyone. Even sickened, watching and smelling the rampage, Corinne had to admit she wouldn't mind breaking some windows, putting the torch to a few cars herself. If she hadn't been flustered forgetting his name, she could have asked Malcolm how his mother was. Why should his destiny bring him round to haul her garbage? Greasy spoons used to post joke signs, reserving the right to serve refuse to anyone.

Table legs suddenly make her feel trapped. Corinne extricates herself and goes to the fridge for three quick breaths of freezer air. Keep in mind that seismic waves occur to relieve deep planetary stress. *If your wife leaves you for another woman, do you really have to hold the door for them both?* Jack would hang a trouble light from a chestnut branch when he needed to work on the car at night.

Corinne retrieves the remote from the mantel, snaps on the TV, and travels the gamut of channels. No one is reporting this after-aftershock. *Oprah* seems to be featuring a woman who, in a dissociated state, stalked herself for several months. Corinne has to flip back repeatedly to glean the mechanics of this: how, unbeknown to herself, she wrote herself threatening letters, set fire to her own house, finally managed to stab herself

Solo Spinout

in the back. An analgesic ad exhorts lumbar sufferers to "put power where the pain is," while down the street a whistling car alarm warns in a mechanical macho voice: "Stand back now. Protected by Viper." There is no one in sight to call this bluff.

Power where the pain is, maybe that was Lela's secret. Through one buoyant midnight snowfall, she drove with the top down all the way home. It must be ninety-five in the apartment, and Corinne begins to suspect her brain of swelling up inside her head. *Some say the world will end in fire, some say in ice.* Once you see them, you don't forget Salvador Dali's thawing watches. On the soaps at least one character eventually goes blind or suffers total amnesia. True amnesty requires both forgiving and forgetting.

At her desk, with a small fan aimed directly into her face, Corinne sits doodling the Müller-Lyer illusion. No ruler required with the yellow quadrille paper—a one-inch line spans precisely four squares. Over and over she amazes herself with how the same inky line can be drawn to appear longer or shorter, depending on the width of angle attached to its endpoints. This eye trick has become as compelling to her as poetry or the runes. It's almost as if through perverse repetition she's hoping to prove that things are, too, what they seem. Corinne proceeds to connect all the careful line-and-angle sets until their random geometric saturation of the page makes her restless.

These days some claim it's pheromones that draw us together, animal odorifics more potent than romance. It's true that even patchouli on Lela didn't smell like patchouli on anyone else. Jack called it musk and asked where it came from, but patchouli oil isn't animal at all. Maybe pheromones orchestrate ménages—natural attraction to the ones attracted to the ones you're already attracted to. Then maybe suddenly nothing smells right. Lela could offer no more plausible explanation for why she and Corinne should convert themselves to "friends."

"I don't want it to be sexual anymore," she said, not exactly mean, but even and aloof. "It's just not what I want."

"You put on a hell of a show," Corinne said. "You certainly fooled the hell out of me."

"I wasn't fooling."

"Then what?"

"I don't know," Lela said. "It just turns out to be not what I want."

Numb and bewildered, Corinne didn't realize for weeks that Jack's turn had come round. Then she waited in patient agony for his confession, which never quite materialized before Lela declared she would take an indefinite break out of town. Abandoned in grief, Corinne and Jack had no source of solace, since they both seemed to have lost both the people they loved. Corinne began sipping whiskey all day, while Jack became obsessed with his body and running. Corinne would awaken hung over at dawn to find him already gone to the track. Every trip to the mall became a quest for the latest shoe, the perfect sock, some collector's issue of *Runner's World*. The clothesline in the basement constantly sagged with damp gray sweats and twisted jockstraps, the recommended antidote for joggers' bloody pee. Corinne could do little but help him load carbohydrates and apply Mentholatum, trying not to nag him for getting too thin.

By the end he was up to eight miles a day, sleeping most nights on the cot in his study. The ostensible point was to run the university marathon in under 3½ hours, and in fact he did it in 3:22, chalk-faced with blistered feet, clutching his side the last four miles. He must have felt he'd proven he could endure anything, but on the short drive home they both sank beneath triumphant cheers into a funk that would not lift. The last photo Corinne has of Jack was taken in his official entry shirt the morning of the race, posing to look lean and mean but striking her in retrospect as mournful and gaunt, skin drawn hollow across his cheeks, sweatband slightly distorting his brow. When she left for L.A. he reverted to golf, the game he had most devotedly pursued before they both got so deep into tennis.

When Corinne wants to remember what a man smells like, she calls to mind the dense intrigue of Jack's rusty beard (though twice she caught there a whiff of patchouli, unmistakably mixed with Lela's juice). She

scoots down a bit in her chair and slides one hand inside
her slacks, withdraws it carefully and extends her fingers
toward the fan, catching her scent on the stirring air
before she licks to taste herself. Why does she think
of jungle when she's never been to a jungle before?
Recognizing an odor doesn't mean you can say its name.
Reportedly typhoid fever makes you smell like fresh-
baked bread.

Corinne and Jack once sat in a tiny strip joint in New
Orleans, watching women strut their stuff along the bar.
Clad only in G-strings, all but one looked dejected or
bored. The one who held their interest was interested in
herself, sneaking little glimpses in the full-length, backlit
mirror, engaging there the eyes of any patron who
caught on to the ruse. This woman had a crucifix tattoo,
Christ's arms stretched out between her breasts. Lapsed
Catholics do have a difficult time, stuck with defying
the concept of sin. Don joked that Lela's behavioral
code comprised whatever would displease her old nuns
at St. Paddy's for Girls. "At least I can get it up," she
shot back. Actually all the "exotic dancers" fared better
in the mirror, less disconcerting once removed. On reflection Lela becomes harder to adore, since, absent flesh
and pheromones, a steely heart may fail to seduce. If
once Corinne was young enough to be captured by
style, lately she has sunk into a quagmire of substance.

At Melrose and La Brea a spacious, black-on-white
billboard says only, in short, thick letters, TRIED IT YET?
Corinne persists in reading TIRED OF IT YET?, though she

caught her own mistake from the first—a recurring, jaded, Freudian slip. The answer feels like *yes* to both questions, whatever product or experience is meant, although, in fact, she's hardly tried a thing—your basically good, if irregular, girl. She once wrote a twenty-page paper on the verb *to throw* and thereby got hooked on the OED. Last night she found herself looking up *jilt*, which started out as a noun for *whore*. How many married couples get jilted together? Computers track everything; there must be stats on-line. Female rats are said to cope with injury more efficiently than males, particularly hard blows directed to the head. It's actually someone's job to harvest ambergris from the large intestines of male sperm whales.

Corinne gulps down a beer before it can get warm. Inside the buzz she decides after all to defrost the fridge, which should go quickly with the door propped open. This hunger for trivial accomplishment strikes her as amusing. Unemployed men may succumb to impotence; unemployed women can drink and clean house. Lela always thought Corinne kept her house too tidy, and Corinne thinks that Lela was right. During Lela's time, in fact, she became even more fastidious, scouring away at her sin against Jack. During the weeks when Jack himself was sinning, domestic drudgery kept her stable enough to endure not only the double treachery but a lame pretense at "friendship" with Lela. Those were the years of the avocado stove with frost-free refrigerator to match.

After Lela jilted Jack and went on her summer hiatus, Corinne became obsessed with improvising hearty meals. Actually, she became obsessed with the fear that the cut-and-packaged side of beef Jack had purchased wholesale the previous spring was on the verge of spoiling in their antique basement freezer. All that hacked-up, putrid cow, lying in wait for her. All that empty time ahead, all that routine necessity to cope. As the meat thawed, it would take on the color of dried menstrual blood, and she would smother it in tomato sauce or mushroom soup, mixing spices to disguise the taste. She began culling dubious recipes from newspapers and magazines, their minor variations blurring on the palate. Jack would sit down to dinner with an air of resignation, both of them humbled by their loss of appetite. Corinne would freeze leftovers for a barely respectable length of time before she felt doggedly justified in throwing them away.

"That beef is fine," Jack insisted. "It's just a bit more aged than what you buy in the store."

"Well, what's the difference between aged meat and old meat?" Corinne taunted him. "There must be some subtlety I'm missing here."

"You'd know if you ever ate any rotten meat," Jack said. "Which I hope you never have to do." Jack was a Depression child, which was why he kept the Coldspot full of food in the first place. Corinne must have been hell-bent on punishing them both.

You're not supposed to use implements to scrape these metal freezers, but Corinne reserves a tarnished table knife specifically for this. Soon her right hand is burning from the ice but feels wonderful on her forehead or grasping the back of her neck. You could never tell for sure whether Lela was igniting you or freezing you out. Corinne arrived at a personal definition of masochism when she realized that both her desire for Lela and Lela's rejection were inhabiting her cunt, forevermore entwined. *So a sadist and masochist get married, and on their wedding night the masochist begs, "Beat me, beat me, beat me," while the ingenious sadist answers, "No, no, no."* On thermograms, surprisingly, pain shows up as cool. The linoleum soon glistens with patches of water, soothing and softening the soles of Corinne's feet. Splashing makes her feel childish. As a girl she played badminton, would giggle if anyone called birdies *shuttlecocks*.

Wrenching, the strategies a couple will devise to avoid each other and the truth in bed. Committee work suddenly absorbed a great deal of Jack's time. Then the marathon training doubled as a fine excuse for months, while Corinne kept on sleeping later and later, then staying up later and later at night. Jack played poker; both of them drank. Corinne subscribed to a series of films, all foreign matinees, alone. Whatever pre-Lela rhythm their life had had was not about to be rejoined. Out of kilter, after a while, turned into the status quo.

If they starved themselves into randiness, they might finish off before misery seeped through, but the least hint of failure made them wary and weary, wary and weary and finally numb. Corinne could not shake the fantasy that an injured animal had crawled beneath the bed to die. She developed empathy for women who fake coming just as "open marriage" got to be a best-selling idea.

The nimblest therapeutic gimmick Corinne has lately heard aims to trick you into REM, awake, in the hope of purging pain. All that's required is to move your eyes back and forth, following the therapist's wand, while you narrate unpleasant memories until they lose their charge. The American way—get over everything. Fix it, recover from it, process it, let it go. This must be the psychic analogue of lighting out for the territory—moving to California no longer does the trick. In the bare dirt yard across the street, two overgrown black roosters have sunk to their bellies, asleep in meager palm trunk shade. So much for the theory of animals on constant quake alert.

Energized by a second beer, Corinne is applying lemon oil to the racket, having salvaged a scrap of cheesecloth from her junk drawer under the sink. The bottle warns: IF SWALLOWED, CALL A DOCTOR BUT DON'T TRY TO VOMIT. Does that make sense? What sense does it make? Corinne is aware she hates vomiting more than she hates the vomit itself. This warm, sweet scent could make her sick, but there's pleasure in seeing the oil darken wood. Clear leather wax will soften the grip.

She's removed an old cowhide satchel from its nail beside the mantel and will try the racket there for a while. The satchel, a five-dollar steal at Goodwill, has hung there for years in place of something framed, cobwebs inside it oddly flecked with tobacco. Almost anything handmade and weathered can qualify for aesthetic display. Does manufactured equipment deserve to be revered? If not *objet d'art*, at least *d'histoire*. Corinne tries hanging the racket by its sweet-spot tear to camouflage the ragged, broken strings, but then she settles the rim itself on the nail with perfect eye-level finality. Flat and straight against bare white wall, the geometry strikes her as preordained.

For the moment she slides the satchel and the Wilson T2000 under her bed. STANDSTILL as stalemate or STANDSTILL as respite. What makes tennis look easy when it's such a hard game? The subtlest variation in tilting the racket can bring on momentous or somber results. Slight loss of control in the angle of swing dramatically alters the fate of the ball. Billie Jean and Martina had superlative wrists, but ordinary players concentrate just to avoid mistakes. A perfect shot can earn you one point, as can any old lousy shot that's in. No wonder hackers lay claim to tennis—once you discount strategic beauty, momentum, and morale, what's left is just coloring between the lines.

Parched air has set floorboards snapping and clicking, especially underneath doorframes. Corinne realizes she's been grinding her teeth and stops. *There's a freeze on useful activity.* She considers a shower instead of a bath but has to acknowledge the futility of both. *A chill wind is reaching you over the ice floes of outmoded habits.* In her final match with Lela, Corinne got heatsick, deep red in the face but white around the mouth. Lela kept asking if she didn't want to quit, and Corinne kept on playing, not answering back. That day the sight of Lela's leather-mesh glove suddenly annoyed the bejesus out of her. Someone ought to study the impact of shame on the vividness of memories. Probably somebody already has, or how emotional charge, at least, determines what sticks to the dendrites in your brain. Once something adheres, it can't be reprogrammed—everything new has to be reconciled. Logically wide-bodies present expanded sweet spots, and it's because they're hollow that composites are so light.

After weeks and weeks away, Lela returned to Granite and unabashedly called Corinne for tennis, as if her duplicitous behavior had occurred outside any impact zone. And Corinne did not suggest that Lela go to hell. Corinne couldn't wait, in fact, to see her back on court, was still deluded enough to imagine they might start over, the three of them, arranging each other more skillfully this time. She can see herself hanging up the dull black rotary wall phone in the kitchen, reaching straight for a nearby pantry shelf where new cans of balls were lined two deep, walking briskly, light-headed, gear in hand, to the car.

"I came back to pack up," Lela greeted her, cranking the saggy golf course net. "I got the job I wanted. The one in Baltimore. How've you been? Did you play the tournament again this year?"

Corinne hadn't known Lela was looking for a distant job. No doubt it was Jack who'd been privy to the plan. But it wasn't Jack Lela asked to see. In the afterglow of disgraceful exhilaration from the phone call, Corinne sustained the announcement like a casual, if potentially fatal, blow. "Baltimore," she said evenly. "Want me to warm you up or go ahead and spin?"

Of course Corinne hadn't played all season and was in no shape for humidity and heat. The asphalt court had softened in the sun (or maybe Corinne's knees were weak, imparting a tricky spring to her step). Somewhere in the first set she ran out of ordinary energy and was forced to call on vital reserves of fury and wounded pride. The feebler she felt, the more aggressively she played, until her game fell into a rhythm of extremes— she would either ace or double fault, pull off a killer drop shot or plunk into the net. Lela must have been nonplussed, since Corinne's failing strategies character- ized her own game at its worst. When Lela finally started rushing the net, Corinne kept slamming the ball at her feet. Corinne was hitting directly at her so often that reflex volleys passed for normal returns. Lela's bal- ance had improved that year because she was bending more at the knees (in an exaggerated crouch that Corinne judged borderline pretentious).

"Gorman teach you to squat like that?" she said as they were changing sides.

"Nasty girl," Lela laughed. "I thought I got it from you."

Lela seemed to have gained control of her style without sacrificing any force, while Corinne had lost her steadiness, her own power working against her. Lela's serve was driving Corinne crazy because she could no longer anticipate what might come: Lela deliberately looked directly at Corinne instead of the spot where she was about to aim the ball. On forehand returns she would do the same thing, shifting her feet at the very last second, telegraphing nothing prior to contact with the ball. Once she realized this, Corinne resorted to a tricky sidespin slice that soon required an elastic band to strengthen her wrist and dull the pain that accompanied each snap.

"Are you all right?" Lela said. "Maybe we should take a break." She was using the hem of her skirt to wipe sweat from her mirrored aviators. The dress appeared dry but reeked of patchouli.

"You must think you've won," Corinne said.

"Suit yourself," Lela countered. "Don't stop till you drop."

"How is Gorman's wife, by the way?" This in a falsely cordial tone.

"I don't know," Lela said. "She doesn't play with us."

"Right," Corinne said. "I remember. She doesn't play with you."

Well on her way to losing a second set, Corinne began to clobber anything she could get her racket on, many a shot brilliantly placed except for landing just outside. All Lela really had to do by then was wait for Corinne to finish defeating herself. Somewhere around 1–4 she slammed a return into Lela's thigh, the sound of it shamefully pleasing. Lela's grimace made her try again and again until she managed a grazing shot that knocked the sunglasses off. "Sorry," she called out. "Take the point."

"I believe the point is yours," Lela said. "The point and the game."

"We ought to replay it," Corinne offered, but Lela was already set to serve.

Corinne "accidentally" hit her again, in the breast this time, bringing tears to her eyes, but Lela wouldn't quit. Corinne didn't even apologize, undeniably cheered by what she had done (*pull down those lacework panties and bite her once through the clit*). When Lela hit a passing shot on return of serve for match point, Corinne brazenly hurled the extra ball into the center of her back. Lela stopped in her tracks and turned around.

"Are you finished?" she said. "You're fucked up."

"I wonder why."

"Oh, come on. I did you favor. At least now you both have to admit that you don't own each other. You better get out of this sun."

Corinne did feel slightly faint, faint with a knotted shriek in her throat.

"We should get something cold," Lela said. "Something with crushed ice. I can go and bring it back."

"No," Corinne said, and she remembers this as her last word to Lela, finally, that simple, blunted *no*. They made their way to separate cars along the rim of the hill, Corinne a few steps behind, concentrating on the auburn braid that bisected Lela's back—the hang of it had made for an easy target. She thinks now how she might have yanked it, yanked it hard, drawing Lela off balance, the two of them tumbling into grass and back down the hill—a scene you might read about on the nighttime soaps.

As Lela neared the MG, conscious of being watched, she executed a little hop-skip step from her repertoire of court moves. She had tucked her glove into the waistband at the back of her skirt, so that with each bounce its fingers faked a wave. Corinne slid into her car quickly, before Lela arrived at the door of her own where she would have to look back, if she were to look back at all. Only after Corinne settled behind the wheel did she realize her legs were Jell-O. Shaded at last from the cruel sun, she watched Lela drive off in the sideview mirror before she opened her door to puke. The tennis felt sleazier than the sex ever had.

This neighborhood has grown crowded with student drivers and driving schools. El Condor Escuela de Manejo is around the corner in a pink frame house. Young

Sun Traffic occupies a tiny storefront two doors south. Latins and Asians of every stripe aim to learn or subvert the rules of the road. Last year one block east three Salvadoran children burned to death inside a locked car, where their mother had put them to sleep for the night. The babies woke early, discovered matches, couldn't escape when the upholstery caught. Homeboys steal cars and set them on fire—Corinne has come to recognize the sound when windows blow. Police helicopters fly low enough to vibrate her stucco building, and she suspects that with searchlights they can see her in her bed. Lately bumper stickers have been cropping up that say DRIVE LIKE AN AMERICAN in red, white, and blue.

Now an ice-cream van is parked beneath Corinne's north window, blasting a music-box rendition of "Send in the Clowns." Several children have crowded in front of the service door, negotiating in Spanish over fruit bars and snow cones, pointing excitedly to colored decals that picture what's available but fail to list a price. In all her years here Corinne has never bought a treat off one of these trucks. She thinks for a moment her time has come, since the beer got too warm when she defrosted, but the idea of putting on shoes holds her back, along with a disinclination toward sweets. Instead she munches a handful of pretzels and transfers three Miller Drafts to a shockingly barren and functional freezer. Dry heat won't wring you out like midwestern humidity, but in L.A. the landscape can burst into flame.

Isn't it rich?
Isn't it queer?
Losing my timing so late in my career.

Jack never wanted to come in her mouth. Really he
did but never let himself. They were snowbound the
day Corinne admitted she would have to leave in the
spring. They wept in sudden bouts for weeks, slept night
after night fully entwined against the darkness and the
chill. Naturally Corinne has always imagined that Lela
compelled him to cream down her throat.

Corinne's first year in California, she kept a journal
of rope dreams—they ran the gamut from nooses to
pearls. Frayed rope, afraid of rope, just enough rope at
the end of her rope. She was roped in and roped off
and didn't know the ropes at all. There was soap-on-a-
rope for cleansing, with solos of "Blest Be the Ties That
Bind." In the tightrope scenes she was less afraid of
losing balance than of the line snapping, less afraid of
the fall than the sound of the snap, since everything
tended to fade before she ever hit the ground. Sometimes it was a circus, more often a familiar, though un-
recognizable, room. Once it was survival training, a
group called Outward Bound. High up between trees
she stood frozen, hands tightly clasped behind her back.
A woman's disembodied voice kept calling out, "I dare
you," while the man who was coaching insisted that
Corinne dance to sag the line. This slack rope dancing
was a brand new art that she seemed already to have

mastered when Jack rang up on the Forest Service phone, demanding to know when the class would end. Her shrink at the time suggested perhaps she had stretched the umbilical cord from Jack about as far as it could go (approximately two thousand miles). Corinne threw herself a symbolic birthday party but got maudlin on champagne and scared, dialing long distance in the middle of the night only to hang up devastated by a drowsy female hello. Of course she saved the journal. How would it read if she dug it out? Psychic archaeology might uncover something she doesn't know, though extraordinary memory can undermine reason—consider the unenlightening feats of certain autistic savants. Orwell claimed that Dali's dexterity extended no higher than his elbow. To Corinne his second most riveting image is the dark, distant outline of a flaming giraffe. Every few years some story appears describing spontaneous human combustion. In that driveway up the street, women keened and wrung their hands, crying over and over and over again: *ninos, ninos, ninos muertos.*

Corinne is examining her remote control, resisting an impulse to hammer it open and expose its magic. There is no way to explore it without demolishing, rather than solving, its mystery. This was the power Lela had, keeping command while keeping her distance, pushing secret buttons in Corinne and Jack, scrambling the signals that transmitted the marriage, keying down the volume till they both fell mute. Corinne catches herself dwelling on this conceit and realizes she is halfway drunk. But she did feel somehow reprogrammed after Lela, no longer elucidated by the concept of *wife*. By the time Corinne left Granite, she had literal trouble breathing in the house, and it seemed to be the house that she needed to leave—six carpeted rooms (even the john) with storm windows sealing everything too tight. *Housewife* has always been a dangerous word—women marrying houses, evolving into *hussies*. Before Lela, Jack and Corinne believed they had passed the ultimate marital test—cutting and pasting broad-striped paper onto slanting, mismatched walls.

The very first afternoon Don and Lela came to visit, Don spilled a mug of beer down the front of Lela's dress, and she asked Corinne for something to wear. "It'll be dry in ten minutes," Don protested.

"I know this comes as a shock," Lela said, "but not everyone grooves on the odor of fermented grain."

The women went upstairs where Corinne carefully selected a close-fitting cotton top and offered her prize-possession shorts, sturdy khakis overloaded with pockets, ordered from a *New Yorker* ad. Lela changed in the bathroom, not closing the door, and Corinne turned away so as not to see her breasts, surreptitiously studying instead the famous Van Gogh feet. That night Lela neatly folded the clothes and left them on a hamper for Corinne to find, patchouli suffusing the fabric, not quite masking animal underneath. Corinne didn't wash the occasionally sniffing at them, imagining the scent had held. It was strangely pleasurable to see Lela in her clothing—if she didn't yearn to be Lela, she certainly yearned to have Lela inside. Maybe Jack thought that bedding Lela would reveal something Corinne needed from him. *Incorporate* is when you have to merge to form one body.

Jack and Lela might both be surprised at her now: beholden to no one, husbanding herself, undaunted by freeways, inhabited by the city. She deciphers maps, gives impeccable directions. And she is fully prepared to proceed alone once Ginger can admit that Corinne is old.

The door buzzer startles and then, repeated, irritates. Only Ginger would likely drop by now, but she has been well trained to knock. Corinne plugs in the telephone as she makes her way to the peephole. A young Latino stares back at her as if he can see her seeing him. He is holding a package or suitcase and seems to be saying, "*Habla usted pollo?*" although that would mean, "Do you speak chicken?"

"Who is it?" Corinne asks. "Who did you want?"

"Pizza," the boy says. "I have pizza."

"I didn't order pizza. Try downstairs." Corinne speaks loudly and overenunciates, but the boy keeps waiting till she gives in and opens the door, which elicits a wide and charming smile. *Guillermo* is broadly stitched in red inside a white oval on his workshirt pocket, though he's also wearing, gang style, a pair of long and comically oversized black shorts.

"Pizza," he says. "Whole pizza four dollars. I will be showing this for you."

"No," Corinne says. "Thank you, but no." As he unzips the insulated canvas bag, the aroma of warm pizza envelops them both. A sample slice is displayed in its own transparent compartment. "God, that looks good," she says. "Where does it come from?" At worst she supposes it's stolen or rejected from a restaurant, though lately there have been recall scares involving cheese from south of the border.

"Pizza," Guillermo grins. "Four dollars this day only."

Corinne finds him a five-dollar bill and accepts the foil-covered, full-size pie, caution suddenly overruled by sheer acuteness of appetite. By the time she unwraps and slices the thing she is salivating like a ravenous stray. She devours the first piece standing at the counter, then sits with plate and napkins at the built-in breakfast nook. The meal in fact is breakfast, if you want to take the word at its word. *He boiled my first cabbage and made it oh so hot. When he put in the bacon it overflowed the pot.* Corinne never heard of Bessie Smith before Jack played that record.

Light is required to view a photograph, but only reminders can illuminate a memory. The pizza tastes, for the moment, memorable. But does the hippocampus record in that predictable a way, sculpting Proustian relationships among discrete sensations? We seem to remember what was painful but not the actual pain itself, not in the way we can call up a song. Women must register childbirth pain less profoundly than the pleasure of sex—otherwise the species might have dwindled long ago. With real seahorses it's the males who give birth, carrying pouches of fertilized eggs. The seedpods of impatiens plants burst open on slightest contact, while their flowers tend to droop and so are known as *touch-me-nots*. Sad thoughts have been traced to the frontal cortex, where a burst of serotonin can resurrect your will to live. This pizza could be the best she's ever had, or at least it could be better than what is yet to come. People claim they'd prefer to die in their sleep, then wonder why they are insomniacs.

Eating has raised the temperature in the apartment another five degrees. Corinne is in the bathroom flossing, never confident in her technique. One indisputable perk of unemployment, this freedom to floss devotedly, hoping for the best. It's plaques on the hippocampus that indicate Alzheimer's, but Corinne is confused as to how this relates to film in the mouth or fat in the arteries. She feels slightly guilty about the pizza, which probably spoiled her appetite for sharing an evening meal. It was Ginger who gave her the Viking runes, which came with a book on the self as oracle. She ought to stop drawing stones at random and focus on an issue, where STANDSTILL may not apply. *Stalemate* is not restricted to chess but hasn't evolved as a pun on tired marriage. Who can bear the mention, much less the vision, of anybody's teeth in a glass? The Morning Star Dairy in Granite still delivered milk in bottles, and you could see the settled nutmeg in their blue-ribbon Christmas eggnog. Once Jack smeared some to lick across her breasts, which made Corinne eager to do the same to Lela, though when she did, it felt so much like nursing that both women got to laughing and nearly lost their edge.

With the hope that it might be slightly cooler there, Corinne lies down on bare hardwood in front of her fake fireplace. She can sense no difference in temperature, but the spot does offer a fresh angle on the racket hung as artifact, all lines and curves, like the game itself, or the shape of a shot as it's put into play. The pathway of your rush to the net should follow precisely the flight of your serve. People take the toss for granted, but Corinne always used it to size women up—any sign of an unnatural toss meant they were likely to throw her off. Of course you have to picture where you want to contact the ball, then toss it up exactly to that point, but Corinne believed this should be done on automatic and had zero tolerance for habitual false starts. Those perky little white dresses back then lacked a pocket deep enough to stash the second ball, subtly implying women were expected to utilize both serves each time.

Commentators emphasize the crucial role of the fast first serve, especially now that radar guns clock everything in miles per hour. But straight off the court top players themselves repeat the adage that still holds true:

Over the long haul and under pressure, you're only as good as your second serve. Each second serve is a test of character as much as it is a test of skill. How quickly can you forgive yourself for having missed the first one? And if indeed you deserve forgiveness, are you worthy of the confidence that's necessary now? Did you misjudge the size of the receiving court, or did your body simply fail to do as it was told? In any case, what on earth makes you think your second try won't plop into the net? Single fault, double fault, all of it your own damn fault.

A truck rumbles by, sending vibrations along Corinne's spine, registering on her nerves as *quake*, pulling her nearly to her feet before she can interpret the engine's rattle. She stands at the window breathing deliberately until the panic releases its grip. You don't hear much talk of foreshocks, a concept perhaps best kept at bay, undefinable, anyway, until it's followed by something worse. As you descend into LAX at night, tennis courts and swimming pools light up the grid. Distinguished by shape and color, geometry undefiled, they have the eerie emptiness of forms that suggest no function.

Across the street one black rooster has bestirred himself, strutting aimlessly about the yard, suddenly crowing with the kind of full-throated effort Corinne thought reserved for heralding dawn. *A whistling girl and a crowing hen will always come to a bad end.* As an inveterate and talented whistler, Corinne took her grandmother's reproach as a complaint about noise rather than a warning about being female. She was well into her twenties before it struck her that hens don't crow at all and that her whistling had been a cocky habit. Grandma Jordan routinely clucked her Baptist disapproval—she held her tongue about Corinne taking up tennis only because it meant she might foresake baseball. There ensued an annoying transition time when Corinne was saving for the racket—no loose change anywhere in sight was safe from her resolute grasp. For her birthday that summer Grandma J. tied a bow around a candy sack of quarters with the unspoken hope it might divert Corinne from her downward spiral to panhandler or thief.

Held now in amber sunlight, the racket is emanating lemon, the odor of which prompts Corinne to check on the beer in the freezer. EVERYBODY HAS TO BELIEVE IN SOMETHING. I BELIEVE I'LL HAVE ANOTHER BEER. This was on the T-shirt of a young male friend of Ginger's who earnestly insisted that AA had driven him to drink. Corinne applies a dishtowel to the hazardous twist-off cap, then takes the deepest pleasure in an almost icy gulp. Nothing compares to the gladdening sound of a tennis ball hit right. In 1953, at nineteen years of age, Little Mo Connolly was the first American woman to win the grand slam. Corinne lifts a giddy but reverent toast. Then she shattered a leg, was forced to quit, died of cancer at thirty-four.

Maybe Lela's destiny was to play the femme fatale, but at what point in life does such a role become ridiculous? With her bone structure probably she is aging well. Smaller-breasted women fare better in the end. It occurs to Corinne that she slammed balls at Lela less for screwing Jack than for discarding him. Then it was just a matter of time before she followed suit herself. She pictures him handsome in the classroom, explaining syllogisms. Sometimes when he wore tennis shorts Corinne would kiss his knees in the car. "Be bold," Billie Jean advised beginners. "If you're going to make an error, make it a doozy."

Corinne has never seen a DEAD END street sign in Los Angeles, only the awkward, euphemistic NOT A THROUGH STREET. Perhaps this is universal now, or perhaps it's peculiar to HOLLYWOODLAND, where realtors have always been hypersensitive to property value semantics. People who live near the sign itself are demanding access for locals only. Ginger's actress friend Sandi just phoned in search of Ginger, having heard she was on her way to Corinne's. This news has made Corinne aware that she doesn't want to see Ginger now. Sandi must be thirty but speaks in the voice of a precocious child. The obvious truth that Corinne has been suppressing is that if she is old for Ginger, Ginger is very young for her, young and still traveling blessedly light. When they first made love this time last year, Corinne apprehended, in the flesh, why middle-aged men gravitate to girls. Nothing mysterious to contemplate, the effort we make to experience effortless youth. But these days the vision of Ginger's lean thighs can make her feel ancient and weary and fat. Not every common malady yields way to self-diagnosis—a pain in your right shoulder can mean you have a gallstone. Corinne imagines a graduate thesis tracing the dangers of looking back, from Orpheus through Lot's wife, on down to Satchel Paige. She ought to ask the runes what it means to grow up and grow old at once. There is that feeling, year by year, that something or other is gaining on you.

It would be cheating, or self-defeating, to remove STANDSTILL before she draws. Corinne resists the temptation, shakes up the bag, and selects a smooth stone, devoid of symbol, which she has never seen before. Its impact is to make her uneasy, as if she ought to have let STANDSTILL stand. THE BLANK RUNE represents the Unknowable. *The Unknowable is in motion in your life.* "Great," Corinne laughs. "At least *something* is in motion." *This rune calls for no less an act of courage than the empty-handed leap into the void. What beckons is the creative power of the unknown.*

Ginger's knock is a vigorous triple tap. Corinne gathers herself on the way to the door.

"There you are." Ginger sweeps past her. "Did you hang up on my machine this morning? Did you want something special? I've been trying to get you on and off. Is this haircut too short?"

"I don't recall now," Corinne says. "Your hair looks perfect, as it always does." Ginger's blond hair couldn't be much shorter, and yet, for her, it's not too short. The women embrace momentarily, aware of each other's sweat.

"God. It's 110 up here," Ginger says. "Sandi and I will treat you to somewhere air-conditioned for dinner."

Corinne takes her hand and leads her to the kitchen, opens up the freezer where they lean in to kiss and laugh.

"You defrosted," Ginger says, impressed. Corinne offers her a beer, which she declines. "You're not supposed to drink alcohol in heat like this."

"You're right," Corinne says, opening a bottle. "Not if you have any sense at all." Ginger's upper arms are tan and toned, verging on outright muscular. She is wearing faded denim with the sleeves cut out, the color accenting gray in her eyes.

"Griffith Park is burning near the zoo," she says.

"God. I hope the giraffes don't catch fire."

"What a thing to think of," Ginger laughs.

Corinne remembers *foreshortening* but lacks the ambition to broach it. "Did you feel the earthquakes?" she asks instead.

"Plural? You're kidding! I must have been driving." Ginger eyes the runes on the table, looks pleased that her gift has been put to use.

"I drew a blank," Corinne tells her.

"That could be good," she says. "Like Russian roulette." She picks up the book. *"Blank is the end, blank the beginning. Pregnant and empty at the same time. Wow. The work of self-transformation is progressing in your life.* See, Corrie, that's good. All the runic deaths are symbolic."

Corinne takes a breath and releases it. "I'm too old for you, Ginger."

"Are you starting that again? You are such an ageist. Fourteen years is not the insurmountable difference you make it out to be. Jesus, it's too hot for this." They move into the living room to sit in front of the fan. "The Poetry-in-the-Schools thing fell through," Ginger says. "I guess I'll keep on at the bookstore for a while."

"I still haven't heard one way or another," Corinne says. "I've been thinking it would be great to work at a 99¢ Store, where the value of everything is level and set. You wouldn't have to worry about ringing up a wrong price. And everybody leaves convinced they've made out like a bandit."

Ginger eyes her suspiciously. "What have you been doing all day?" she asks.

"Marinating in my own juices, I guess."

"That I believe," Ginger says, then notices the racket on the wall. "What *is* that?" she says. "Where did the new antique come from?"

"My ex," Corinne says. "Husband, I mean. It's the racket I had when I was a kid."

"I believe it," Ginger says. "It looks so . . . innocent."

At this Corinne tears up.

"What did I say? What did I say? I'm sorry for whatever it was."

"Nothing." Corinne stops herself. "You're right about not drinking beer in the heat."

"I never knew you played tennis."

Corinne fetches the trophy from the bedroom, which Ginger examines in disbelief. "I never even knew you played at all, and you turn out to be a champion. I thought you were just a Martina groupie like every other dyke in L.A."

Corinne laughs, looks at her tenderly. "Believe me, I never played really well. But at least I was athletic enough to fake my way on court."

"Teach me," Ginger says. "Teach me the basics. Teach me the basics, and we can play."

"I don't think so," Corinne says, taken aback by this impossible proposal. Last July Ginger came over for "Breakfast at Wimbledon." Corinne fed her strawberries. They drank champagne in bed. "I want you to go on up to Ojai without me this weekend," she says. "Go on with Sandi and whoever else. I want you to give yourself a chance to meet new people. We both need to meet people our own age."

"You're depressed," Ginger says softly. "You've been cooped up here all week, worried about the job. You'll feel better after dinner, after you cool off."

"I'm not depressed, dear heart, just realistic. But you two go on to dinner. I've already overeaten." Probably Ginger can smell the sausage, offensive to her vegetarian soul. "I'll give you a call tomorrow," Corinne adds. "Maybe the Los Feliz will be showing something good."

"So why did the guy send the racket?" Ginger asks. "I've been wondering that myself."

Ginger is stroking the trophy, slowly, with the inside of her thumb. "He must still love you," she says, and Corinne smiles to think it might be so.

The evening stretches out, breezeless now and hazy, some new pressure system having brought the smog back in. At least this is creating a brilliant purple sunset. Children are riding bicycles, calling out Spanish names. Across the street Corinne's neighbor Arturo is hosing off his old yellow pickup, a custom number, carpeted, with wooden benches bolted down in back. He once gave Corinne a ride to school and got embarrassed when he saw her staring at the centerfold shellacked inside his glove compartment door. On a car radio at the stop sign, someone has turned up *Lay, lady, lay. Lay across my big brass bed.* Corinne distinctly remembers her realization, the first time she really heard these words, that she could feel Dylan singing them to her at the same time she felt herself singing them to Lela. *You can have your cake and eat it, too.* Researchers now claim people "remember" events that never happened at all. Old Bobby Bodeen told her on serve she should snap out her arm like cracking a whip. This may have been true, but neither of them knew the manner in which a whip should be cracked. Blue-collar kids weren't supposed to play tennis, but Willow, Illinois, was a blue-collar town,

About the Author

Ann Nietzke's novel, *Windowlight*, won a PEN/West Award for Best First Fiction. Her short stories have appeared in *Shenandoah, Other Voices,* and the *Massachusetts Review.* In 1995, *Natalie on the Street,* her portrait of a Los Angeles "bag lady," was among six finalists for PEN/West's Nonfiction Award. Other nonfiction has appeared in the *Village Voice, Saturday Review, Cosmopolitan, Playgirl,* and *CALYX Journal.*

Nietzke is a recipient of a Creative Writing Fellowship from the National Endowment for the Arts and Residencies in Writing at the MacDowell Colony. She has an Master of Arts in English and lives in Los Angeles.

Date Due